SUMMER QUEEN

AMELIA WILDE

Hey, Serena—

Check this out.

1

Before

SILVERY BELLS CHIMING against glass shouldn't strike terror into my heart.

They're bells. Harmless.

But if I'm being honest, my heart was struck by terror a long time ago. My mother did it, over and over, with all the precision of a blacksmith banging a sword into its final shape. The difference is that I turned out thin and soft.

I'm not a weapon.

That makes me breakable.

It especially makes me breakable for people like

Luther Hades. Remember, my mother said to me before I got on the train to come to the city, *if he finds you, you'll wish you were already dead.*

Because he'll kill me, I repeated back for the thousandth time.

Worse. Then she pressed my suitcase into my hand, gave me a fierce kiss on the forehead, and gave me into the keeping of my very own security team.

The security team is not here now, which is probably why my heart is racing, the beats uncontrollably fast and impossible to slow.

This is the thing my mother warned me about. Going off on my own. I'm doing it, and I'll probably pay for it. I always do.

"Persephone." My best friend Magda nudges me with an elbow. "Are you okay? You look pale. You aren't going to throw up, are you?"

I am not like the other girls at the boarding school in the city. I'm not even like Magda. I call her my best friend but I'm certain I'm not hers. We're from different planets, and mine's the kind of planet that can summon me home without a moment's notice.

Her, on the other hand?

She has three credit cards from her father and looks like a nymph sprouted from a combination of an elegant, polished-wood library and a fashion magazine. *She* looks like she might conceivably be allowed to visit this off-campus mystic shop called The Fates.

Magda wears a navy sheath dress and a silver necklace, her hair swept back into a gleaming ponytail. You could mistake her for a Kennedy or an actress. Or both.

Whereas I am stuck wearing my school uniform. The only thing it has in common with Magda's weekend outfit is that part of my uniform is navy. That part is the navy sweater vest that's too warm in the late September heat.

"Seph?"

The others are already ahead of us so far that the bell chimes again, its sound muted by the glass. Magda blinks at me.

"I'm not going to throw up," I say finally. "Let's go."

We push our way into the narrow shop against a weak wave of air conditioning. The bell on the door chimes again. Three times, three chimes. It doesn't mean anything—it's a bell on a door. But I can't relax.

The shop seems normal. I don't have a lot of experience shopping in stores because that's always been absolutely forbidden. The city had been forbidden until a little over two years ago.

As winter rolled into spring I found it harder and harder to get out of bed.

No matter how many soups my mother made and how many thick chunks of bread she brought to me, I got thinner. She pinched and threatened and begged and finally I did something dramatic—I told her that I would die if she didn't let me go to school.

By the time fall came I was on my way into the city, accompanied by two huge men who would live in the building across the street and watch my every move. Except today.

I've lost them for this one, single outing.

The potential fallout of this—losing school, losing everything—is like acid in my throat. If my mother discovers that I've put myself in danger she'll make me come home. No discussion. Those have always been the terms.

I run my fingertips over a row of crystal necklaces on silver chains, their meanings on neatly printed papers beneath each display. One for strength. One for calming. One for optimism. I could use all three right now.

Jewelry. Books. Rows of small boxes on the shelves —tarot cards. Jill and Amy have already gone toward the back of the store. It's a surprisingly long room. It looks a lot smaller from the outside, but now that I'm through the door it looks like it goes on forever.

A woman appears from nowhere, and it's only after she's out in the main store that I see the doorway behind her. A beaded curtain hides the next room.

"You're here for a reading." There's no lift in her voice. It's not a question. And she's looking straight at me.

My stomach turns to ice and my face to fire. She looks…ageless. Like she could be twenty-five or fifty and there's no telling which one is true. The woman wears a gray… what is it? Magda would call it a jumpsuit. The word "jumpsuit" doesn't do justice to how elegant it looks, from its thin straps to the wide legs that flow around the woman's ankles.

"I'm not." My voice sounds too loud in the little store and Jill and Amy turn to look at me. Their eyes shine, and I can't tell if it's because they're interested in a reading or because they're waiting to laugh at me.

I can never tell. I'm trying to speak the language of the other girls in the boarding school, but at the beginning of my third year I still feel like I'm only fluent in linen dresses and planting my mother's flowers.

"She is." Magda's firm. No nonsense. She steps up and threads her arm through mine. "Come on, Seph. Let's see if there's vomit in your future."

Two other women come out of a room to the side.

They don't wear the same thing as the first, but the outfits are similar enough that they look like three flowers together. Never mind that flowers aren't usually gray. Their clothes are the soft color of ashes on white petals, almost a fawnish gray.

It's deceptive, somehow.

I know it is, even if I don't know why.

Magda tugs me forward and motions to the other girls. *Come with us.*

Jill and Amy don't hesitate. This is a show for them but it's something else for me. My skin knows it. My heart knows it. *Run, run.* This fortune holds danger for me. It holds truth.

There's no running with Magda's arm through mine.

The three women disappear behind the beaded curtain and we're close behind them. The beads aren't beads, I realize as they slip through my fingers—they're rocks. Small, black rocks. Like something carved out of the side of a dark mountain.

Like the mountain that watches over my home.

The side room has two halves. One is mostly taken up with a round table big enough for four people to sit at. The other half is storage. It's almost too familiar. Wooden shelves, wooden baskets. My mother would use the same things.

Does she know I'm here? Does she sense it? Is she coming to put an end to this even now? Most of me is horrified at the thought of her finding out, but a small part, a tiny, weak part of me longs for the safety of her bruising grip.

"We should go," I whisper into Magda's ear.

She gives a sharp shake of her head. "I want to see this."

"I don't have any money for a reading."

"I'll pay." Magda flicks her eyes toward me, then the table. "Little Seph, always so clean and pretty. Always so perfect. I want to know what's going to happen to you."

I don't. I have the tingling, knife's-edge sense that what these women have to tell me isn't something I want to know. My throat feels too tight to contain my heartbeat. If my hair could stand up against its own weight, it would. My wool-blend skirt itches against my legs with every step Magda makes me take until I get to the seat at the table. Jill and Amy hang back but Magda stays, a hand on my shoulder. Why does she want this? There's nothing about me that could possibly interest her or anyone else.

I've lived a boring, isolated life. It's far from perfect.

The three women take the other seats at the table.

For the life of me I can't tell if the one who holds the cards is the one who spoke to me before. A shimmering quality takes over my vision. Good. This is going to be the moment when I pass out in this weird little shop and my friends have to call for help. The security team finds out I'm missing, and my mother finds out I'm missing, and then I'm dead or trapped back home, which is basically the same thing.

The woman with the cards passes them back and forth in her hands, watching me. Magda's hand tightens on my shoulder.

"The future," the woman says, and the other two nod their agreement.

"Doesn't Persephone get to pick?" Magda sounds so innocent, but I know it's an act. She's not. Not really. Not the way I am. I'm pretending to be worldly and she's pretending that these women aren't absolutely in charge.

The woman with the cards meets Magda's eyes above my shoulders. "Sometimes the cards choose."

She looks back to me, and I have the sensation of the sun dropping down too close, lighting up the sweat gathering at my hairline and the pounding pulse in my neck for everyone to see. Then she half-rises from her chair and places the cards on the table in front of me.

"Persephone." She settles back in her seat as she tests my name. I wish I knew hers, but I bet it's something secret and strange and wouldn't make me feel any safer. "Shuffle the deck."

I feel, rather than see, Jill and Amy move closer in.

My hands feel oversized and clumsy on the cards. They're old, worn smooth by lots of readings. What if I threw them all up in the air, right now, a little explosion of papers and fortunes? It would blow up the tension in the room, at least.

I shuffle the deck.

Three stacks, two stacks. It's folding more than shuffling—folding the cards in on one another like I'd fold egg whites into a cake batter. It doesn't seem right to riffle them the way I would for a new game of solitaire at home, so I don't.

The cards can't actually be hot under my hands, can they? No, no. It's only me and my nerves. My heartbeat is louder than any clock I've ever heard.

"Done." I put them back in the center of the table, as far as I can reach. "I guess."

"The future," the woman intones, and picks them up with an easy lift. Her eyes settle back on me. She must know I'm not supposed to be here. She must be able to see it in my face. "In order to read your future, we need guidance from the cards on who you are now."

She turns the first card over.

Everyone leans in.

The bright image on the card could be me. My mouth goes dry at the details—the simple dress the woman wears, sunlight beaming down on her face. She leans out over the edge of a cliff, arms thrown open wide. She's going to fall.

"The Fool." She lifts a hand to tap the card. "A blank slate. A new beginning."

I feel like a blank slate. A blank person. It still stings a little. The fool? All of the cards she has in that deck, and the fool is what I get? Fine. Fine. I don't need to get worked up over this. They're only cards. Maybe I am foolish for coming here.

"What's to come," she says, and I can't take my eyes

off that fool, that innocent fool who has no idea she's about to tumble off the edge. Or maybe she does, and she's fine with it.

Another card.

A lightning bolt tears through the frame to a tower of stones. The image is the act of striking, pure energy throwing the walls of the tower to the ground. I can feel the shake and crash as stones shear away and tear into earth.

"The Tower can mean liberation." She considers it in its spot next to the fool. "A sudden change. A destruction."

"A destruction of what?" I can't stop myself from asking. "Of me?"

"It could be," Jill chimes in. And to my horror, the rest of the women around the table make sounds of agreement. "It could be anything. And everything."

Anything? Everything? It could definitely mean my school career. Coming here could be what triggers the destruction of my only freedom. It could be worse than that, even though right now school feels like everything.

"Consequences," the lady snaps. "And for whom. The final two cards."

The first one she flips over is Death.

Wings. Bones. Darkness, like a shadow over everything. My heart stops.

"A metaphorical death." She purses her lips. "But possibly a physical one. As relates to..." One more card. The card shows a queen, and it's my mother. It could be my mother. She has the same regal pose as her, the same set to her jaw. She stares out of the frame of the card, defiant and steadfast. "A queen. A mother figure."

My lips have gone numb, my fingertips aching.

"Do you know this person?" The woman's soft question cuts to the quick.

"My mother? Of course I know her."

Amy lets out a short laugh and swallows the rest of it back.

"The cards are saying I'm going to have my world destroyed? I don't understand. You're saying that my mother is going to die?"

The woman traces a hand around all four cards.

"You are at the center of these cards. Without this little fool here, none of the rest is in motion."

A hot flush of anger, followed by a guilty, wretched hope. "So it's my fault."

"There's no fault in the cards. Only cause and effect."

"She's not going to die." I look her in the eye. This shadow of a queen, this fortune teller in a city shop, she—she's not real. This isn't real. But she looks back at me as steadily as the woman on the card. "And definitely not because of me. Like—what? I'm going to kill her or something? That's crazy. I would never do that."

"Never is a long time," she says, and picks up the cards.

I stand up, fast and hard enough to rock the table. "You're a liar. A cheat."

Except it doesn't feel like the truth. It feels like I'm the liar. I'm the cheat. I'm the one who's going to kill my mother, who I love, love, love. I love her, don't I? Except sometimes, when her fingerprints are there, purple and blue on my arm, I hate her.

I barely make it out of the shop before my stomach

clenches. My knees land on glittering gravel. I throw up in hard, wrenching spasms that last for ages. That's how the security team finds me—kneeling in the alley, my mother screaming over the phone.

2

HADES

Four years later

PAIN IS A STRONG HAND. A fist, unrelenting.

A vice around my temples made from bone and diamonds.

Everything I've ever done puts the force of itself around my eye sockets and the back of my head, drilling in deep. If I could be in the dark, I would.

But fuck if I'll walk away from the bright glare outside the sterile operating room two levels above the mines.

Not until they tell me if my dog is dead.

I've been standing here for minutes or hours. An eternity. At some point in the distant past I considered sitting. Fuck that. I am not a superstitious man. I don't have time in my life for mysticism and wonder at the workings of the universe. Yet a gnawing at the pit of my gut warns me away from taking a seat. It would feel like giving up.

Dr. Martin sweats underneath the strings of his surgical mask. The back of his neck gleams. The man must know that this is the most important surgery of his life. How could he not? He knew the terms when he signed his contract. His services in exchange for another life. Somewhere, in this mountain, someone might have told his wife the stakes. Or perhaps not. She doesn't matter to me.

Conor's blood left a hot stain on my hands. The unbelievable gall of that fucker. To betray me twice? *Twice?* He might as well be Zeus.

The thought filters down through the pain circling my skull. There are things I need to keep the knife's edge at bay. None of them are here, outside the specialty operating suite I had built with the knowledge that it would probably never be used. Who the fuck would have the balls to come into my mountain and shoot my dog?

Other than my brother.

Dr. Martin's team surrounds the table, heads bowed over the anesthetized form of my dog.

Another pain taps at the back of my mind. It's a steady beat, like a dripping faucet. There's a certain pleasure in feeling it. Pain, properly felt, is fucking extravagant. But there's more extravagance in the denial of it. It's an old habit. I won't think about other dead dogs and other bursts of loss, each one its own neutron bomb. They all left radiation hanging in the air until those parts of my memory were unlivable.

This is unlivable.

There's no more viscera on my hands, but it left its imprint on my sleeves. My shirt. It hurts to bring my own reflection into focus in the surgery window.

It's an image of a haunted man.

My heart drives blood through my veins in a violent drumbeat. Deny it, deny it. Deny the urge to tear down the operating room and leave nothing but rubble. That won't get me where I need to go.

Where the fuck do I need to go?

The answer filters through my pain like an icepick, chipping away at a frozen core. If Conor was with me now, that dog would be fucking frantic. He'd throw his body against my legs until I moved. We're well past the time when a warning could prevent this—prevent any of this. Perhaps it was too late to change course months ago. I remember the moment. My office. Conor growling. The words that slipped by my own denials.

I have torn rooms apart. I have torn people apart. But I couldn't tear apart my own desire for Persephone without killing myself in the process.

Maybe I tore her apart, too.

Sick worry explodes in my gut, a land mine made of bile and rage. Where the fuck is she? Where did he take her? Who paid him more than I did?

My fist hits the glass with earth-shattering force.

The glass is reinforced, bulletproof, and it holds. Dr. Martin's shoulders go up toward his ears but his hands don't stop moving. What the hell are they doing? It was one bullet, not a hail of them.

One of the nurses looks up, says something to him,

looks back down. I can't hear anything but my own heartbeat. If Conor doesn't have a heartbeat, I will raze the city to the ground. I'd do it for less. I'd do it for Persephone.

Zeus did this.

Ah—there it is. The knowledge that's been circling my brain like a buzzard. Of course he didn't pull the trigger himself. He wouldn't dirty his hands. But he set it in motion.

He paid for it.

Who else would have the money, or the inclination?

Most of the people here fear me and worship me in equal measure. How could they not? I'm the reason for their lives. That's what it is to sign a contract with me. Zeus and I have many contracts between the two of us. The most important one is unspoken. It's a cold war. He doesn't attack my mountain, and I don't attack his businesses.

Something changed.

I slam my fist against the glass again, and this time there's a faint crack from one of its edges. I'm stronger than reinforced glass, even with pain slicing its way through my brain and radiating down the back of my neck, all the way to the base of my spine.

"Mr. Hades."

"What could you possibly need right now?" It doesn't occur to me that my teeth are gritted until I have to answer Oliver. His reflection appears next to mine in the window. "I've given orders not to be disturbed. Do you have a fucking death wish?"

"It's been a long time." Oliver sounds gruff. Why?

I rip my eyes away from the surgery to find him offering a pill bottle.

There is only one occasion that I let myself slip in front of Oliver.

It was five or six months ago at the end of a long period of unrest in the mines. A late shipment from Demeter set all of it off. It set everything off, didn't it? I could kill her. I should have killed him for knowing about me then, rather than feel this... exposed. I think of killing him now, just for the suggestion—just for the idea that I could be weak enough to need what's in that bottle.

A bitter rage burns my throat.

He's fucking right, isn't he? A bloodbath in this hallway wouldn't prove him wrong. This is the consequence of having a so-called inner circle. Inevitably errors are made. Inevitably knowledge seeps through the cracks. The walls come tumbling down.

I snatch the bottle out of Oliver's hand.

It's a relief to feel the smooth, plastic shape of it in my palm. Fuck him. Fuck Oliver, and fuck all the people in that operating room who are making me wait in this light.

One pill—that's all it takes. It goes down easy, because it always fucking does. That's the nature of things a person needs, even if they're poison in disguise. These pills are not poison. They are an illusion.

It doesn't feel illusory, the way the pain releases its grip and flees. The way the room comes back into focus. The way my heart stops its jagged throes and calms the fuck down. I drop the bottle into my pocket. Until Conor's better again—and he had better fucking get better—the bottle will have to be with me constantly. No more mistakes.

Oliver stands at the edge of the operating room

window, watching me. Of all the people in this mountain he's one of the few who has the courage to look at me directly. It's a risk, and he knows it. Lucky for him he's lived a lifetime of frankly insane risks. I'm just one more.

"What happened?" My voice is hoarse.

He shifts. Puts his hands in his pockets. Glances into the operating room without flinching. He wouldn't fucking flinch. He's seen worse than a dog with a bullet wound. "I reviewed the tapes. Every single one of them."

I say nothing.

"The maid was involved—she led the way. Got her out of the room and brought her to one of the workers from the mines. He had a gun, which—" Oliver inclines his head toward Conor, through the glass. "I don't know what else he was planning to do."

It wasn't just any worker, was it? It was a specific worker. I can see him now, standing on my factory floor, his head yanked back while I dip my fingers between Persephone's legs.

More pain, this time not from the light, from my head. It's deeper than that. It's like a wave lapping at the shore. I'm the fucking shore. The pain is an ocean. I'll never swim out of it. Not until I get her back.

"He took Persephone."

"Yes."

"The maid?"

"Gone. The cameras lost her on the platform."

The maid. Persephone's maid, the one who brought her food throughout the day and helped her dress. Dark hair, dark eyes. She wasn't plain, was she? In the right outfit, with the right makeup...

The scar running down Oliver's face stands out, redder than usual.

I stand up straight and put one hand in my pocket. Oliver already knows about the fucking pills, clearly. He had the good sense to bring them to me alone. No one in the operating suite has so much as turned in my direction, so I don't need to end their contracts over this.

"What do your people in the city say, Oliver?"

He has as many men in the city as I do. More, probably. It's one reason he's exceptionally useful to me. A crazy motherfucker like Oliver inspires a kind of loyalty. I'd rather expend my resources here. And I'll have to, because the mountain has been compromised. There is a crack in my defenses. There has been theft. Theft of the worst possible kind.

"A group met them when they got off the train." He takes a deep breath, though I can't imagine why he'd be nervous to tell me what I already fucking know. "Zeus's people."

The firm boundaries that have kept Zeus, Demeter, and I from killing each other all these years crumble and fall. He's gone too far. Too fucking far. And if he's willing to do that, then I'm willing to retaliate using every goddamn weapon I have.

Dr. Martin stands up straight and hands something off to one of his nurses in a flash of metal and red. I do not have fucking feelings about my dogs. That ended for me a long time ago. But a certain numb horror comes over me as he strips off his gloves and tips them into a biohazard bin. He goes to the sink and hits the switch for the water. He washes Conor's blood from his hands and wrists. There's no help for the surgical gown. I want the window to shatter so I can feel the shards bite into my own skin.

Oliver moves back and Dr. Martin comes forward. Will I kill him over this? It's a possibility that lives in the ache of my hands and the tension across my back. If it's bad news, then I might answer with my own bad news. It would be a breach of contract.

Letting my dog die would be a breach of contract, too.

The door to the surgery opens and Dr. Martin steps out into the hall. It's the one place in my home that I've allowed to be white, and only because the sterile environment requires an exceptional amount of bleach. Pill or no pill, it hurts to be here.

Dr. Martin tugs down his mask with shaking hands. My heart barely beats. Inside the operating room the rest of the team in their blue scrubs move back and forth in a sick dance around the table. What the fuck are they doing? Covering him for burial or making him comfortable for recovery?

"Mr. Hades." Dr. Martin rubs the back of his hand

over his forehead. "We've cleaned Conor's wound and repaired the damage to the muscle tissue from where the bullet entered."

I restrain myself. Instead of lifting him off the ground by his neck, I only dig my hand into the front of his scrubs and twist, pulling him close enough to smell the disinfectant and soap clinging to his skin. And then, and then, I fucking can't ask the question. It stalls on the tip of my tongue and digs its heels in, refusing to come out.

Will he live?

Dr. Martin's eyes widen, his face pales, and for the third time today—tonight—whatever the fuck time it is—someone else is looking in where they shouldn't be. Someone else is seeing the things I never wanted anyone to see. His heart beats wildly in his chest. It feels like it's making direct contact with my knuckles.

He takes a deep breath. "He'll be all right, Mr. Hades. Conor is going to make it."

I shove him away. He'll be well compensated. Him and his family. His whole team of surgeons and nurses. They belong to me. Here in this fucking mountain, I own more than diamonds. I own *lives*.

Just not the ones I want. Never the ones I want. Conor could have died. And Persephone? She might already be dead. *No.* The pain sears my eyes, my head, my whole goddamn body. It blinds me more surely than the sun.

I force it back. Pain is a strong hand, a fist. A vise.

I'm stronger. "It's time to leave the mountain."

3

PERSEPHONE

My eyes are dry.

With men closing in around me and Decker backing away, it seems normal that I'd cry. Appropriate, even. But that only happened on the train and with Hades. A switch has been flipped, and here, on this platform, not a single tear falls. Is it because I'm courageous, or is this shock? Warm air swirls up from the platform, laden with summer humidity. This isn't how I wanted to come to the city.

For a moment I can breathe. For a moment there's space between me and the men. It shrinks and shrinks until finally one of them reaches out and takes my arm.

They've been waiting for this—to see if I was going to fight back. The hand above my elbow makes me sick, it makes me nauseated, but what am I going to do? What am I going to do? Terror is cold, like ice, like snow. Every breath is sharp.

Another man comes alongside me and takes my other arm. Then it's a hustle through the bright lights of the platform building and out the other side. Into shadow. Into darkness. Each heartbeat is a call to run, run, run. Get out of here. Get free. But my thoughts won't line up in a neat row. Or else they're too neat. It all makes too much sense.

Decker had to get paid. Decker sold me. How long has he been planning this? From the very first time we met? No, that can't be right. Can it?

The men surround me on the sidewalk. It's a clear night and even amid all the tall buildings the air is alive in a way that it wasn't in the mountain. In the mountain, everything is tightly controlled, from the temperature to the mines. And me.

I can't think about it too much. It'll make me fall apart. It'll make me collapse onto the concrete and sob. I shouldn't want to go back there, but I do. A bird shouldn't want to live in a mine.

And why, *why*? I want to go back to a man who made me sign my life away to him in exchange for Decker. I want to go back to a man who put his hand around my throat and his fingers between my legs and made me come in front of his entire factory floor. I want to go back into the dark, where he hurt me, where he ended me, where he made me finally live.

I do.

Because there was something in his kiss. There was something dark and wretched and hungry. I wanted it. And he wanted me. There was something pure about that desire.

A big black car comes down the street and pulls up at the curb. The men tighten their hands around my arms like I'm going to make a break for it. Where would I run to? There are four of them, plus Decker. There's nowhere to go.

My pulse crawls, then runs, my heart shaking the bars of its cage. How did it come to this? All I wanted was to be free. All I wanted was to visit those lions outside the New York Public library. All I wanted was to stand in the sun and not have anyone's hands on me. Not my mother's. Not Decker's.

Things have changed since then.

Now I want one person's hands on me, but Hades isn't here.

A scream catches in my throat and I swallow it, the sound as sharp as broken glass. I have to hold it together, at least for now. Holding it together is the only way I'll live through this nightmare. The city is dangerous. That's what my mother always told me. Buildings loom over us, the black car gleams in the night, and I am trapped in a circle of men who could do anything. Anything. My lips are already numb. My fingertips will be next.

My lungs will freeze, unable to get a breath, and then—

One of the men steps forward and opens the door.

The other two shove me forward. No, no. I twist in their hands, struggling to get purchase on the sidewalk. I was going to cooperate, make it easier on myself, but I can't, I can't. One of them claps a hand over my lips and gives my face a violent shake.

"Not so hard." The voice from inside the car is

surprisingly mild. "It won't make as good a gift if you damage it."

The man grunts and lets go of my face. Then they're lifting me, setting me into the car. My head goes under the doorframe. This is it—this is the last moment I could have escaped. I squeeze my eyes shut in spite of myself. There's no point in seeing who did this. Is there?

I open them again.

A man sits on the other bench seat in the back of the car, facing me. But he's not looking at me. He's looking down at something in his hand—a phone, or a small tablet—and the light from the screen caresses his face.

He's gorgeous.

There's no other way to describe him. Languid and luxurious, in clothes that were undoubtedly made for him. Charcoal pants. A white dress shirt with the collar open. He's unbuttoned in a way that Hades never was, but it's...purposeful. The hairs on the backs of my arms stand up.

I've read books before, illicit books, that describe characters as tall, dark, and handsome. I don't know how tall this man is but from the way he fills out the seat, my guess is...tall. Almost as tall as Hades. But where Hades is clean-shaven, this man has a dark fall of stubble and dark curls to match. Curls that seem barely contained by his precise haircut. How old is he? My mother's age at least.

I find my voice. No more sitting here in silence. No more.

"I'm not a gift." The phrase falls flat and awkward, a bit shaky. Not how intended.

He looks up from his tablet and smiles. Perfect teeth. Glittering eyes. It's the most charming thing I've ever seen, and the second most dangerous.

"You're conscious, then. That's good."

"Who are you?" I am not going to let my voice shake. I'm not a little girl anymore. I might have been when I stepped on that train, but enough has happened since then to make me a woman. It has. "I don't know what you think you're doing, but I'm not—I'm not property that you can take and give."

He considers me, using one finger to flick off the tablet. The light goes away, leaving his dark eyes visible by the lamplight.

"I'd venture to guess that you are property, Persephone. I'd venture to guess that you signed a contract in recent days. Did you not?"

How could he know?

"Anything I sign of my own free will is my business, not yours."

"Your mother would beg to differ."

My mother doesn't have anything to do with this. Or she has everything to do with this. If she'd let me have a life, I wouldn't have had to make plans to escape from her. Either way, I'm not going to discuss her with this stranger.

"You don't know anything about my mother." My palms are slick on my lap. "I'd appreciate it if you'd let me out. Right now."

The man tips his head back and laughs. "Into the city? By yourself? That would be an insane thing to do, especially when I have something so valuable."

I seize on it. I can't help myself. "That's right. I am valuable, which means you should put me back on the train."

"The train to where?" He sits up and balances his

elbows on his knees, closing the distance between us. "My sister's compound or my brother's mountain? Which one, little Persephone?"

His casual, mocking tone stings…and then the meaning sets in.

"Your—your brother?"

His *sister*.

Horror fills my mouth with bile. I'm going to throw up. If they're siblings, that makes Hades my uncle. And that can't be.

That smile flickers over his face and stays, getting wider. "You didn't know," he marvels. "How could you not have known?"

"We didn't discuss his relatives." An old instinct for honesty stabs me in the back. I tried for scorn and missed by a mile. My thoughts race, chasing each other, tangling up together until it's impossible to tell one from another. Hades' brother? I can't imagine him having a brother, or parents. Maybe he would have told me about them if there had been time. There wasn't time. Or he didn't want me to know. I hold it together through sheer force of will.

"What did you discuss, if not family ties?"

Punishments. The things a slut like me would moan and scream for. The way he would ruin me. The way he did. I discussed things with his mouth and his fingers. His cock. "That's none of your business."

The car pulls away from the curb. My body tenses, getting ready to throw myself at the window, but of course I don't. I'm frozen here in my seat with a man Hades never warned me about. Why would he? He had no reason to think I'd ever be here. I had no reason to think I'd ever be here. We both thought I'd be trapped in the mountain.

He's frowning at me, that man. Studying me. It's the kind of expression that hides more than it shows. The kind of handsome I know instinctively not to trust.

"I'm sure your mother won't be happy to hear that you spent so much time discussing...things with Hades." The pause tells me he knows exactly what kind of discussions we had. "I suppose it was too much to expect restraint from him."

"What does it matter to you?"

It takes forever to look him in the eye, and another forever for him to smile again. Handsome. Relaxed. If I didn't know better I'd think he could be kind. A low laugh, easy and warm. It's nothing like the bitter shards of Hades' laugh. If I'd met a man like this first, I don't know what would have happened. Terms like better or worse don't seem to apply.

"It's not nice to give damaged gifts. Exactly as I said before. And I have a suspicion that if I examined you, I'd find one small part of you missing. Your hymen."

A lurch, a fall. The floor of the car isn't steady any longer. It's tipping in front of me, rocking back and forth. An unsteady ship. No part of me longs to go back to my mother's fields. Maybe I did when we were speeding past in the train, but now? Now?

The blood drains from my face.

The thing about running away from my mother is that I knew I could never go back. Never. She might have warned me about Hades, she might have warned me about bad men in the city, but if he takes me back to her?

She's the danger.

I can't think about what will happen. The locked doors. The months of silence. The hard glances and harder slaps—I can't. If he takes me back to her, I won't survive.

A memory comes back strong enough to draw blood. A back room in the city, a woman with cards. A tower falling. Do you know this person? Magda's hand on my shoulder. I'm not going to kill my mother. *That's crazy. I would never do that.*

My world has already been destroyed and remade. The cards told the truth.

I'm the thing that set all of it in motion, just like that woman in gray said. I'm the little fool. Is my mother the dangerous one, or am I? A sudden ache at the back of my throat and the center of my heart makes me sit up straight, trying to relieve it. If she had only been able to love me, really love me and not possess me the way she did, none of this would have happened. The cards never would have fallen that way.

"Don't take me back to my mother." A broken whisper. I no longer care what it sounds like. "I don't know who you are, but I know you can't possibly be that evil."

He offers his hand with a flourish that makes my heart skip. I take it because what other choice do I have? "How rude of me to totally neglect our introductions when we'll be working together so closely." His other hand taps lightly against his chest. "Everyone calls me Zeus. Even my sister, though she usually prefers names for me that have a bit more bite. I'm sure she'll tell you all about me, now that you've been enlightened."

He drops my hand. His sister. His brother. I'm speechless. Betrayed. She never told me. She spent all those years forcing me to look at that mountain and whispering horror stories in my ear, but she never once let the truth slip. I'm more like her than I realized.

Zeus drops my hand. "Perk up, Persephone. We're here."

4

PERSEPHONE

ZEUS'S PROPERTY—I'M assuming it's his—could not be more different than Hades' mountain lair. Hades' home and his mines and all of his other secrets are in a place blasted from black rock shot through with gold. It's night incarnate. And even though the sky is pitch dark, this building shines. It glows. Enormous windows take up most of the first floor. Frosted glass allows light out, but doesn't let me see in. My heart beats wildly. Zeus's smile hides secrets. I'm sure of that. His building must hide even more.

But he's proud of its facade. Miles and miles of white marble, soaring into the sky. If Hades lives in a fortress, Zeus lives in a castle. A castle transformed into an elegant city building and planted on the corner of a block. It could take up the entire block—I have no idea. I wouldn't be surprised.

Zeus reaches back into the car, hand extended, a true gentleman. My legs shake, weak, which forces me to lean on his hand. We walk together between two planters of flowers. The blooms are a riot of color in the golden light of the streetlamp and I have a sudden twist of homesickness. The last time I saw this many flowers it was because I was in my mother's fields.

I miss the fields. I don't miss my mother. Unless Zeus is lying—and I don't think he is—then I'm not sure I know her at all.

Two men wait in sharp uniforms in front of a pair of huge double doors. The doors are a solid white, like the rest of the building. The men step forward and open them for us in a smooth, choreographed motion.

And inside...

It's a party.

That's what it has to be. Music spills out onto the sidewalk, music and warmth and the low hum of people chatting. A woman laughs, the sound contagious, and my mouth twitches reflexively. Suits and gowns are briefly visible in the open doorway, bathed in more warm light. A man at the other end of the room leans over a woman on an antique sofa, pressing kisses to the hollow of her neck. She tips her head back to give him better access and I think of inching my thighs apart for Hades in the black of the bedroom he gave to me. How did this get so out of control? How did I never see all the ties between the people I knew? They were there, all along, and I was oblivious.

Zeus repositions his arm and my hand, and now he's escorting me in. Hot shame trickles down my back. I look completely foolish. The women in here are in short gowns with plunging necklines, fabric that shines in the light, and I'm wearing what is essentially a bathrobe with buttons. I'm barely dressed.

A four-piece band plays in the corner of the room. A woman with a violin is the centerpiece and the music threads itself through my heart. It's nothing like the pop music we used to listen to when I got to go to school, and nothing like the folk songs my mother insisted were the only things worth listening to. Sensual. That's what it is. It's sensual and upbeat, and the violinist seems lost in it.

"Zeus, you're missing the party." A woman with bright red lipstick approaches and extends her hand. Zeus bends over it and kisses her knuckles. What is he doing? Is this really a thing people do? Maybe if you're as gorgeous as this woman is, with her dark hair in a shining wave and her dress showing off every curve of her body. Her bright eyes turn on me and I'm swept away in another flush of embarrassment. Her hand drops down to my face and she traces underneath my chin. "Did you bring us a new plaything?"

Zeus laughs easily, but his arm tightens to his side, taking me along with it. "Not a plaything. A guest. So you have to be nice to her."

"Oooh. But can't we play with her while she's a guest?"

He gently removes her hand from my face. "No."

"Why not?" She pouts, her cherry lipstick perfect. I haven't seen anything that bright since the poppies in my mother's fields and the splash of red fabric in the closet Hades made for me. "They enjoy fresh meat. If I'm honest, so do I."

Zeus catches her wrist in his hand and brushes his lips against the fine bone there. "Shouldn't you be playing elsewhere? You have a lot of admirers here tonight."

"They tip better if they're jealous." She winks at Zeus and turns away, hips swaying with every step. The back of her dress plunges so low it takes my breath away. One wrong move and she'd be completely exposed. Maybe that's the point of it. I follow her path through the couples leaning breathlessly into each other and waiters with trays balanced carefully on their hands, the single women in tight black dresses and bright jewel tones, men on the prowl...

"What is this place?"

Zeus glances down at me. "My business, little Persephone."

"Your business is parties?"

A smile quirks the corner of his mouth. "You could think of it that way."

I don't want to think of it that way—I want to know what it is. The evidence is right here in front of me, but my brain can't connect the dots. Frustration rises, hot and choking. I'd give anything for the cool of Hades' mountain.

But Zeus leads me farther into the warmth of the room. I feel his attention shift away, though he keeps me close. He's scanning the entire place. I steal enough sidelong glances at him to learn that the charming smile never drops. People see it, and react to it, like they're bathing in sunlight itself. It's different for men and women. We pass the four-piece band and go into another, larger room.

"The lounge is only the beginning of the party," Zeus says. "It continues throughout the building. Into the back. Into the bedrooms."

This room has a series of low tables tucked into alcoves, each one with its own overstuffed booth. Light glitters at the edges of shadows. The couples here are eating, drinking, talking close in the booths. *Did you bring us a new plaything?* What did she mean? A new wave of fear tightens around my ribs and squeezes, making it hard to breathe. Zeus brings people here to become playthings. It must be common enough for that woman to assume it. He could drop me at any one of these tables, any one of these couches, and then what? Would the men without a woman circle around me?

What is Zeus' business?

"It's not really a party." I chance saying it because impending doom is creeping in with every step we take. There is an end to this stroll we're on. There has to be.

"Of course it is. Don't you see all these people enjoying themselves?"

A couple cuts in front of us then, the man growling, the woman laughing. He has his hands tight around her waist, so tight that her dress is hiking up. It could be above her thighs soon. Nobody seems to notice or care that he's practically stripping her down. Nobody, aside from Decker, seemed to care when Hades pinned me to him and finger-fucked me in front of all of his workers.

"I'm not supposed to be watching this."

Zeus stops and takes my face gently in his hand, turning it up so that I have to look into his eyes. He's got dark eyes, shot through with caramel streaks that look like they could be pure gold.

"No. You need to see this. You need to understand. It's true, Persephone. You're here as a gift to your mother. But you're also here as a gift to you."

Tears spring up in the corners of my eyes. This is not a gift, no matter how convincing he sounds when he says it. I don't let the tears fall. I won't.

"There's nothing here that I want."

He bends down then and turns my face away. Zeus has a soft touch. I don't see how he and Hades could be brothers. I don't see how my mother could be his sister.

"Look." I close my eyes. "No. Look." His grip tightens, and there it is—that familial resemblance. My heart skips. A soft touch doesn't mean he's less dangerous. A soft touch could mean he's far worse. A man with gentle hands in public doesn't have to be the same behind closed doors.

I don't want to risk what might happen behind closed doors, so I look.

"There. See? Nothing so bad as all that." Zeus guides my head so that my eyes have a moment to linger on every booth, every sofa, every chair. All of them are occupied by a man with a woman, or a man with two women. Their hands glide along each other's bodies. The women laugh, low and lovely. "You were right on one count."

He smells good—fresh and clean, like someone you'd want to be close to. It's distracting in a number of horrible ways. I tamp down the instinct to ask him how I was right. I keep my lips pressed firmly together.

"It's not a party," Zeus admits. "It's supposed to be like one for the clients. I don't like an atmosphere of secrecy. My clients shouldn't get the impression that their pleasure is a dirty thing. The federal government says it is, but whoever listens to them?" He laughs, and the sound blends in with the music and the chatter. There are other sounds, too—the background music for all the rest. A breath, catching. A soft, needy moan, almost a whine. The word *please*.

Who is making the money here?

Zeus. All of it flows to him. That's what it means to own something. But he can't be the only one providing services here, because he has his hand on my jaw and nobody would pay to see that. Nobody would pay just to see that. I'm certain of it. And it can't only be that the servers are making money, because a dinner club would be...for dinner. It wouldn't involve so much whispering and stroking and....

"Ah," Zeus says. "You understand now."

"The—the clients are the men?"

He moves my head a quarter-turn. "Not all of them."

In the last booth on the right, a woman in a flowing black jumpsuit, her hair pulled back away from her face in an indestructible chignon, leans in to the lady with the cherry lipstick. The jumpsuited woman strokes a hand through the other's dark hair. The intensity in their faces doesn't feel like a purchase. But that's what it must be. Red lips purse and pout and then, with a turn of her head, she suggests going somewhere else. The two of them stand up and move quickly toward a hallway at the back of the room.

"You sell women to your clients?"

Zeus puts a finger on my lips. "Oh, no, Persephone. They sell themselves."

5

PERSEPHONE

ZEUS TAKES me to the very back of the hallway and produces a card from his pocket. He slips it into a slot on the wall and the silvery panel there opens with a whisper. A private elevator.

Why would I need to see a place where women were bought and sold? What could that possibly teach me that I don't already know? I've already given myself away, more than once. I can't bring myself to think about the alternative too deeply.

The alternative is that he wants me to understand his parties, and his business, so he can sell me himself. It's sickening to think about. All those strange men, with their strange hands...

Hades was a strange man, a small voice whispers. He has strange, rough hands, and the things he did to you are worse than anything happening in that lounge...

The things he did were worse. And I begged for them. Don't go too far down that road, Persephone. It'll only end in heartbreak.

We ride the elevator up, up, up and it lets us out into a wide hallway with plush carpet, all of it bathed in bright lights. Hades would hate it. Tables line the edges of the hall, each with a big bouquet of flowers. It must be meant to look like a hotel—a high-end place. But it's not. I remind myself again and again. That's not what this is. It's not what it seems to be.

He stops at the second-to-last door on the left and opens it.

"For you." Zeus gestures me in.

As far as prisons go, it's lovely. A big bed with plush white sheets. A lamp glowing on the bedside table. Through one open door, there's a bathroom with an oversized tub. A chair by the wide window. A view of the city.

A view of the mountain.

It's far off in the distance, but even from here, it seems to take up the whole horizon. The sight of it pierces my heart. Why? Why? I don't want to go back there. I want to go to New York City. That's where I want to go. But I can't make this latest development turn into another step in my plan. The plan has been shot to hell and left for dead.

"I have to get back." Now Zeus is all business. "There are clothes for you in the closet. You'll be comfortable here."

I won't.

He turns to go.

"When are you sending me back?"

Zeus winks, becoming the charmer all over again. "We'll see."

He closes the door behind him and I can't help myself. I run for it, keeping my feet light and silent on the carpet. My hand meets the cool metal of the handle, a flare of hope—

It's locked.

He's locked me in.

You'll be comfortable here.

I'm going out of my mind, out of my soul. I don't know whether my mother was right or wrong. Whether it's my fault or hers, or Hades or Zeus. I don't know why nobody will tell me what's going to happen, and I hate it, I hate it, but I'd rather be in that mountain than here.

I want these clothes off of me.

Why do I want him? Why do I want that mean, broken man in the mountain more than I want to be here, or home? What kind of person does that make me? And will it matter if Zeus sells me off anyway? He said I wasn't a plaything. That might be because I'm an asset.

One of the buttons pops off the robe and I tear at my nightgown, kicking off the shoes. Get off, get *off*. Lillian put those clothes on me knowing that she was sending me here. She knew what she was doing. Where is she now? She could be dead. She could be downstairs, one of Zeus's women. It doesn't matter.

I fill up the enormous bathtub and climb in while the water's still hot. The burn is a pleasant torture and I let it touch every inch of me, every wanting inch of me. Because even locked up with Zeus's prostitutes, even without a hope in the world, one awful thing is still true.

I want his cruel, heartbreaking brother.

6

PERSEPHONE

I FALL ASLEEP LATE, wet hair splayed on the pillow, to the sounds of people fucking on either side of me. Their moans and cries sink into my dreams. My dreams become the soul-searing night that Hades ruined me. I want it and I hate it and I need it, and I wake up the next morning with aching thighs from pressing them together in my sleep.

In the bright sunlight I try every window, every door.

I run my fingers along the crown molding, as if a secret latch will appear.

One of the heavy chairs would probably break the window if I managed to throw it, but that would make enough sound to draw everyone's attention. It would also be a twenty story drop down to the concrete. I want to escape. Not die.

It's at least mid-morning when I give up and slump on the bed again.

Nobody disturbed me last night. Only my dreams. But someone will be coming soon. One night they will, and I'm already questioning whether that person will be Hades. It was so terrible and intense and real with him, but it could have been a dream, too. This could all be an illusion.

The clothes in the wardrobe are meant for whores but I pull them on anyway. Lacy panties and bras. A silk dress with a neckline so low it almost shows my nipples. It's that or the clothes I was wearing when I got here, and those seem stained with betrayal.

I'm brushing out my hair when a knock sounds at the door.

It's Zeus, there in the hallway in a fresh suit. "Sleep well?"

The sight of him jars the confusion out of me. No more feeling sorry for myself. No more. Done.

"Do you always care so much about your prisoners?"

"You remind me of Demeter when she was younger." He arches an eyebrow. "I hope you don't think you're a prisoner here, Persephone. This is only a temporary arrangement."

"You locked me in last night." Anger stirs, growling. "Why would you lock me in if I'm not a prisoner?"

"For your protection." Zeus looks completely sincere. "I go to great lengths to keep my clients in line, but I wanted to be absolutely sure no harm would come to you."

"You sent someone to steal me. You're lying." My voice doesn't tremble at all. "How is that protecting me?"

"I saved you. From my brother, who is far more dangerous to you than I am." Understanding comes over Zeus's face. "Oh, god. You did more with him than sign a contract, didn't you?"

"What I did is none of your business."

Zeus steps forward and takes my face in his hand, looking deep into my eyes. Searching for something. My heart flies up into my throat.

"Perhaps you're damaged goods after all," he says thoughtfully. "Look at that. You think you want him. Tell me, little Persephone. What did he say to you to convince you that he's not an evil bastard who'd just as soon kill you as kiss you? Or had you not worked that out yet?"

I yank his wrist down so he can't touch me anymore.

"I think you're jealous of him." I've never had siblings, but I've read about them. Jealousy is the one thing all siblings have in common. "You wouldn't—you wouldn't talk about him so much if you weren't jealous."

Zeus bursts out laughing, and if I didn't hate him so much it would be the most intoxicating sound in the world. He laughs like nothing has ever gone wrong in his life. He has a beautiful, melodic laugh. Zeus throws his head back and it's like he's been kissed by the sun.

"Jealous? Of his sad little life, all holed up in his mountain? No, I'm not jealous. Who could be?" His laughter settles, tapers off. Zeus clears his throat. "You'll have to excuse me. That's the funniest thing I've ever heard. No, my relationship with my brother, such that it is, doesn't inspire jealousy. It might be better if we didn't need a relationship at all, but that's not how the chips have fallen."

"Do you pay your women in diamonds, then?" I cross my arms over my chest. I'm not wearing this dress for Zeus.

"Aren't you a clever one?" Zeus reaches down to press a fingertip to my nose, and my entire body recoils. What the hell is he doing? "No, I pay my employees in cash. Diamonds would be cumbersome for them. Less so for me." He sighs. "Our government, in all its wisdom, frowns upon businesses like mine. I'm shocked that your mother didn't explain this to you. She uses Hades in much the same way."

"So things will be heated when he comes to get me."

Zeus actually covers his mouth. It does nothing to hide his grin. "Hades won't come here, sweet, innocent Persephone. He can't."

That, more than anything else Zeus has said, makes the floor feel unsteady beneath my feet. I can't imagine my mother striking a deal with Hades and I can't imagine Hades being dissuaded from anything. Zeus just sounds so confident. He's *sure* Hades won't come here.

The ghost of a thousand whispers echoes in my ear. If he finds you, he'll kill you. My mother wouldn't make a business partner out of that kind of man. Would she?

I want to scream.

"You didn't come up here to ask me questions about my mother," I tell him.

"Right," Zeus says. "I came up here to tell you that you'll be coming downstairs this evening."

To the party. To all those men, scenting all those women. A thin line of sweat breaks out underneath my hairline. "I'm not coming to your party."

"Oh, you are." Zeus goes down the hall with a long, graceful stride. He turns his head halfway down. "You're the guest of honor."

7

PERSEPHONE

PANIC RAGES IN MY CHEST. It's a storm I can't calm, one that touches every part of me. My lips go numb. My hands go cold. My chest tight, the pressure unrelenting. Guest of honor? No, no, no. I can only imagine what that means. How is this nightmare coming true? Once I read in a book that we spend all our time worrying about the things that never happen. The real problems are the ones that take us by surprise. I never worried that I'd be a prisoner in a whorehouse. Not ever, not even when Decker and I were making plans for escape.

Another knock on the door sends me lurching for it without thinking. If it's Zeus again, I'll attack him. I will.

It's not Zeus.

The woman with red lipstick stands in the hallway, a metallic case in her hands. I look like a wild thing with half-brushed hair and a prostitute's dress. She looks as elegant as she did last night, with more muted lipstick and a comfortable outfit. I'd kill for those leggings. I want her flowing top. When she sees me, her face falls.

"Oh, no. You look so sad—are you all right?"

I shake my head, once, twice. I can't stop.

"Come here, honey. Sit down."

She guides me to a chair by the window and presses me into it. Brings me a glass of water. Makes me drink. Then she crouches down in front of me and looks me in the eye.

"I'm Aurelia, but everybody calls me Reya." Her smile is as warm as Zeus's and strikes me as genuine. "I'm sorry if I upset you last night. I thought you were another girl joining the ranks." Plaything. That's what she called me. "They pay more for fresh blood."

"I'm not fresh blood," I say numbly. "I didn't want to come here."

She purses her lips in a gorgeous frown. "Life gets hard out there. I know. Trust me, we all do. Thank goodness we have Zeus. Anything I can do to help?"

Life gets hard out there? What is she talking about? Her tone implies this place is a refuge. There's no way it can be. Women are sold here. It's just dressed up in silk and satin. I shouldn't be confiding in this woman—Reya. I don't even know her.

The truth swims up and bursts out. "I won't be here much longer."

"You'll be here tonight, though." She pats my hand and smiles. "Zeus thought you might want some help getting ready. I always like to do it early in case I make any mistakes."

"This early?" The thought of sitting around, dressed up and waiting for Zeus for the rest of the day, makes me vaguely nauseous. There's also a nagging memory of what getting ready meant when I first arrived at the mountain. "How long is this going to take?"

Reya cocks her head to the side and grins. "Longer, when you account for lunch." A knock at the door punctuates her smile and makes it even brighter. "Speaking of, there it is."

I swear I'm not hungry, but as soon as she opens the door and pulls a tray inside, I discover I'm ravenous. Last night, before Lillian woke me up—it was only last night—Hades took me. He made me his. And we didn't linger over dinner afterward.

Reya and I linger over lunch. She is the first person in years to treat me like a normal person would. Except she's not a normal person, and this isn't a normal situation. It is not normal to sit in a skyscraper of a whorehouse eating BLTs with a prostitute. Still. I put the food in my mouth and eat it, and it dampens the raw hunger and anxiety. Food has a way of doing that.

By the time we're finished with our second course— tea and cookies, for some reason unknown to me— the sun has wheeled overhead into the afternoon. Reya brushes the cookie crumbs from her hands and stands up from the edge of the bed. She retrieves her metal case and drums her fingernails on it, an impish light in her eyes.

"Buckle up. It's time to make you look good."

EVERY SWIPE of makeup makes me more nervous until, at the very end, Reya has to unhook my nails from the arms of the chair. "You're good, sweet pea." She steps back and surveys her work. "Zeus will be pleased."

She goes to pull another dress out of the wardrobe and helps me step into it, fastening the zipper behind my back. This one at least reaches the floor, but I can tell from the air shifting in the room that it's got a low back.

"Is that a good thing?" I swallow hard. "Why am I asking? It doesn't matter what he thinks. I don't even know why he wants me at this party."

She laughs. "To show you off, obviously. You're his new prize."

Show me off. To the people at the party? It must be. It must be some scheme to prove to my mother that he's brave. That he has something on her. That he's not afraid to take his daughter and tell the world about it. His world, anyway. Why would he need to do that if he's going to give me back to her? If they both use Hades, whatever that means, then maybe they also use each other. Suddenly the train comes back into focus. It runs from Hades' mountain to my mother's fields to the city. It's a lifeline. It's a knot, tied tight around the three of them. But knots can always be undone if you pull the right cord. Zeus is trying to tighten it.

That has to be his plan.

And if that's his plan, then he might have a secondary plan along with it. He might be trying to...to reinforce my mother's fears about what will happen if I'm allowed to be in the city. He wants to show her that her worst nightmare is real.

I have to get out of here.

The window isn't an option, and when I try the door it doesn't open. Please, I think wildly. Someone come get me. *Someone come save me.*

My prayer is answered a moment later. The door opens from the outside and Reya sweeps in, a minor goddess in a deep blue. How can she just unlock the door like that? Is it freedom she had to earn by pleasing Zeus? The thought sends another quake through me, through the floor, through the world. I do not want to go down to Zeus's party.

It's a bad idea. A very, very bad idea.

Reya doesn't give me any choice. She hooks her arm through mine and pulls me along with her. We're headed for the elevator. We're headed for god knows what.

She pats at her hair and puts on a big smile. "Time to make our entrance."

8

PERSEPHONE

THERE ARE OTHER ROOMS.

Of course there are other rooms. Zeus is a king in his own castle, and a castle isn't just a lounge and a pseudo-restaurant for prostitutes to woo their clients. He also owns a ballroom, which is where the gathering tonight is.

Zeus meets me at the entrance and takes me neatly from Reya's arm. Everything seems too bright, too harsh. It's just candlelight and sconces on the walls, along with some lit-up centerpieces at the tables ringing the room, but it seems like the blaze of high noon.

"Tonight's a bit different," Zeus murmurs into my ear. "I've brought guests."

"You had guests last night."

"You're right, little Persephone. But tonight I'm hosting an event for some local policymakers."

It's impossible to tell which men are clients from last night and which men are *local policymakers*. They're all wearing dark suits. Zeus must like a dress code. All of them look weak compared to Hades. All of them look small. But they outnumber me by far. And they must know...they must know what Zeus does here.

No wonder my mother was afraid of the city.

If the people in power support this business, then they don't care what happens to me. Why would they? They're here to have a good time. I might be here to give them one.

Zeus mingles his way through the crowd, shaking hands, pushing me forward at every opportunity. He doesn't give my name but he lets everyone get a good look at my face. I never checked the mirror after Reya was done with me. I could look like anything. I'm hoping I don't look like myself.

At the other side of the room a low dais looks down over all the revelers. Two antique chairs perch in the middle. Oh, god. Zeus really thinks he's a king, doesn't he? There have never been any consequences for him. He kidnapped me, and not a single person in this room will bat an eye. He can do anything. He can yank on the ties that bind him to my mother, toy with her, terrify her....

And he can do worse to me.

We take the seats.

A man dressed in simple slacks and a black shirt bends down low next to Zeus, a silver tray in his hands. Zeus lifts them with a nod and hands one to me.

I don't want to drink it.

Whatever it is, I don't want to drink it. My mind is trying to separate, to hide from whatever this situation will become, but my body knows the danger. My heart punches at the inside of my ribs. My vision sharpens, taking in hemlines and stubble and dappling on gowns.

The party moves around me, time slipping by. It gets louder. More raucous. Men appear at the edges of my vision, watching.

"Drink," says Zeus, and his voice has taken on a

sharp edge. His smile reminds me of predators in the dark wood. "Relax."

Relax? For what? I lift the heavy glass to my lips automatically and take the tiniest sip. Zeus is still watching. I take another sip. It's sweet. Light. The aftertaste is odd, but what is it? *What is it?*

"A sheltered girl like you could use some experience." His voice is a low lie in my ear. "Look around. You could take your pick."

This should scare me, shake me to the bone, but my heartbeat seems oddly slow. I don't recognize this calm. I'm used to the cold wash of anxiety. This feels warm. Too warm.

"What are you talking about?" My tongue feels thick in my mouth. "I thought you didn't want— didn't want to return damaged goods."

"Getting fucked once or twice isn't damage. You can even get compensated for your time."

More dark suits, more men. More shadows. None of them is the shadow I want. It's hard to sit up straight. It's hard to stay on the edge of my seat. Why is it so hard?

"Did you put something in my drink?" I can't even

muster up a glare for Zeus. I'm thinking of Hades, and I'm thinking of how many men there are and how there's nothing between me and them. How Zeus could give me away with a wave of his hand. How he might do that. How it might be better for me if I just give in and let it happen. Let one of them take me upstairs. Let one of them—oh, god. My stomach twists, turns, but my body feels somehow distant and too close.

"I wouldn't do that," Zeus says mildly. "Nothing to harm you. Just a pinch of something to help you relax. Something to help you enjoy the party."

No. What I need to do is get up and run. Get up. Run. I lift one arm off the chair. It only moves a few inches. I take a breath and summon more strength and swing my feet above the floor. That's not running.

"See? You're having more fun already. Now. There are quite a few men who have expressed interested in meeting you while you're available. A couple of women, too, if you'd rather—"

I don't get to hear what I'd rather do because there's a loud sound from the far end of the build-ing. Down toward the lounge, toward the street. It beats back against itself until there are a thousand crashes all happening at once.

"Fuck." Zeus stands up inhumanly fast, too fast for me to see. I shake my head and try to focus.

It's chaos. A chaos of bright gowns and dark suits sprinting away from one another. Men in vests with guns weave through the crowd, scattering people. Guns? Vests? The police. I've only ever seen them from a distance. Back when I was in school, I saw— I saw people like this. Police mean something bad is happening. Something terrible is happening for Zeus, and I'm going to get caught in the crossfire. Handcuffs glint in the light. There are so many officers in what must be bulletproof vests. What goes on here that they think they need bulletproof vests? A fresh horror pinches and pulls at my skin but I can't do anything about it.

And then, in the middle of everyone, I see him.

Hades.

Half a foot taller than anyone around him. Eyes black, depthless. The other men in here aren't wearing suits, they're wearing rags. Hades wears black as deep as his eyes. Every step he takes creates more space around him. The policemen pull away.

Women flee. He's not a charmer, like Zeus. He's here for me.

I'm holding my breath. I only discover it when my lungs start to ache. The first rush of officers arrives. I'm useless next to them. Nothing. They surround Zeus and all talk over one another, or maybe it's one of them talking with all the echoes of whatever was in that drink. I hear *human trafficking* and *prostitution* and *right to remain silent*.

They haul Zeus away, hands behind his back. Distantly, something shatters and cracks. Glass or something harder, or perhaps it's whatever twisted tie remained between Zeus and his brother.

The man who is here for me.

The officers drag Zeus off the dais straight toward Hades. I thought the two of them couldn't possibly be brothers, but as Zeus comes level with Hades he leans out, using the grip of the officers for leverage, and says something to Hades. Zeus's charming grin remains in place. Hades answers him, jaw set, a casual fury on his face. Neither of them flinch or cower. They're almost exactly the same height.

Then the moment is ended with a yank from the officers and Zeus walks with them, no resistance, head held high. He's still the consummate host of the party. It takes a long time—too long—to focus back on Hades. He draws nearer and nearer and finally he blocks out the light from the ceiling.

He crouches down in front of me, if you can call it that. It's as elegant a movement as I've ever seen a person make. There's almost no blue left in his eyes. He looks so strange and different here. Too powerful for the room around him. Too lethal. Over his shoulder I watch three separate officers change their minds about coming to talk to me.

Hades puts a huge hand on my knee. I feel like I've reached out and grabbed the only solid thing in a storm. The high winds stop tearing through the room, leaving it still. A dangerous energy arcs between us, as tangible as electricity. Whatever has happened here tilted the world on its axis. I just don't know how much yet. Maybe I'll never know.

"Did he touch you?"

The question drops from Hades lips like he's asking about the weather, or if I prefer chocolate or vanilla. The hairs on the back of my neck pull straight. I'm an ancient emperor at the coliseum, giving out a death sentence. Or a life sentence. The lie is so tempting. If I tell it now, then Hades will kill Zeus, never mind the police and the other people. I can see it in his eyes. There would be consequences to that, though—consequences I can't see, no matter how long I look. I don't know how the board is set. I don't even know all the pieces of the game. I don't know anything. When Zeus called me little Persephone he was right.

"No."

Hades shoulders relax a fraction of an inch. He does not let relief show in his face. Maybe he doesn't feel it. Maybe there's no relief to be had when you're in a war. And he is, isn't he? Zeus has started one. Or—*or*—they've been locked in battle for years. I didn't know. I just didn't know.

It's the police who circle now, held at bay by Hades. He hasn't said a word to any of them, and he doesn't now as he bends down to pick me up in his arms. He's solid rock, untouched by the wind, and I can't help myself. I put my arms around his neck and hold tight. He says nothing but his heart beats hard and fast.

THE EYES of Zeus's private security never leave me. I can feel them burning into my skin on the way out of his whorehouse. It's surprisingly nice, given what an obnoxious fool he is. Not to my taste, of course, but not altogether disgusting. *This is a mistake.* He was so casual when he said it. Smiling. That motherfucker. He only has himself to blame for what I've done tonight.

I'm surprised they don't shoot me. It would be easy enough to do it now, when half the city's police force is in here arresting prostitutes and clients. Easy enough to blame one of the trigger-happy cops. But they don't. They're likely in shock. What I've done is shocking, if only to our fucked-up little family.

There are certain lines we don't cross. The most important one is that we do not interfere with each other's business. Zeus only skims off Demeter's products in the agreed-upon amount. I keep his company on my payroll, a fiction of numbers and spreadsheets. And Demeter makes the things we need and sells the rest.

All of that is rubble now. It must be. Unless I can get Demeter to understand, which is unlikely. Her fields still burn, the smoke rising in thick curls to the sky. She has to stop or she'll kill us all.

It's also possible that I've killed us all.

For love? I don't know if I'd call it that. It's baser than that. More animal. Persephone belongs to me, and Zeus took her.

Light batters my eyes on the way out of Zeus's building.

"Where are we going?" Persephone whispers against my neck.

"Home."

She relaxes. Where else did she think we'd go? I'm going to close the doors to the mountain and bar them for good. I'll send a courier to meet Demeter.

I'll figure it all out later, when my heart stops racing like a runaway horse.

The upset I've caused in Zeus's place has spilled out onto the sidewalk. Some of his whores cry and argue with the police. A few of them are walking away as fast as they can in high heels. I don't care. Persephone—her warm, alive, untouched body—is the only thing that matters to me right now.

A car waits at the curb. As a rule, I don't drive. These were special circumstances. I pass by five additional officers running into the building, open the passenger door, and drop her inside. Persephone rests her head against the window. Pressure mounts at the back of my neck. We need to get the fuck out of here before Zeus's people get themselves together.

The steering wheel feels unfamiliar in my hands and the streetlights are knives boring into my brain. No time to dwell on it. I yank the seatbelt over Persephone and click it into place, then head for the train platform.

It's making an extra stop tonight. Fuck getting on with anyone else.

We abandon the car at my private platform. On the

way to the train—it's coming, I can hear it—Perse-phone blinks and stirs against me.

The scent of her, hidden underneath a perfumed soap that's wrong, so fucking wrong, has set my heart back into rhythm. And it's a dangerous one. It knows no boundaries. It's wild with life and pain and anger, things I spend my life trying to keep at bay and fucking failing.

The train rolls to a stop, hissing, clanking. The moment we're inside it jerks back into motion.

Thank fuck. The lights in here are ones I can toler-ate. It's too late by now to ease the worst of the pain but I don't fucking care. I put Persephone on the sofa and her head lolls back. But then she blinks, seeming to wake, her huge gaze focusing on me. He's dressed her up like one of his whores—dark lipstick, smoky eyes, all the things meant to attract the kind of men Zeus wants favors from. I've ruined his plan.

"He put something in my drink," she whispers. That confused, lost look should soften me. It has the opposite effect.

I thread my fingers through her hair—someone's

changed it, straightened it—and pull her head back. If Zeus has done anything, it'll be on the slim line of her throat. One glance tells me there's nothing. It's her eyes I'm concerned with.

And yes, Zeus has put something into her drink. Persephone's pupils are wide and black, almost like mine. I shouldn't touch her. I should tuck her into bed and let her sleep it off.

No fucking way.

Her pulse beats at the side of her neck, breaths shallow from between parted lips. She's already arched her back for me. As far as I can see, she's all right.

It's not enough.

I stand her up, brace her hands on my shoulders, and rip the dress away from her. My skin is on fire. My heart's not beating, or it's beating so hard I can't contain it. I need to fucking know. I am not a man who needs. Who gives in to desires. For her, I am. *This is a mistake*, Zeus said. It wasn't a fucking mistake. It was an escalation.

A killing rage blends with animal desire in a mix so

potent it almost carries off the driving pain in my head. My father tried to stamp these things out of me. I tried to follow his lead. I didn't try hard enough. These feelings take the form of Persephone, a living woman, here in my car.

She's wearing lace underthings I've never seen and the hot spike of jealousy that roars through me at the sight of them touching her skin is enough to melt the train to the tracks. Persephone gasps when the panties come apart in my hands, then the bra— shredded, nothing. And then I put my hand around her neck where it belongs.

Need overwhelms. Overruns. I tip her head back and inspect her. Jaw. Neck. Breasts. Her nipples peak, hard and wanting. If there's so much as a scratch on her I will turn this train around, find Zeus in his jail cell, and crush the life out of him. My hands ache. She smells so fucking pure, so innocent, and she is not. I have fucked her, I have made her mine, and another man tried to take that from me.

It's searing hatred and equally searing relief that drives me on. I haul her off her feet, pull her to the desk, force her open. I need to see every inch of her.

I need to feel it, too. I shove three fingers inside of her, my hand still around her neck, and find her wet. Wanting. I stretch her, punish her, look into those big, black eyes and let her see me.

"You signed a contract," I growl into her mouth. "That contract does not include wandering off in the middle of the night." I pull my fingers out and deliver a sharp twist to each of her nipples. She whimpers, cries. I can feel the vibration through the palm of my hand. It's mine now, that sound.

I open her wider, lean her back, expose her. Humiliate her. It's too wide, there's no way she can hold this position, but she will. For this, I need the light. It's a rare fucking occasion. She sucks in a breath. One silvery tear falls to the desk. Yes. Fuck. Yes.

She can't hide from me. With her legs like this, pinned, I see everything.

Everything.

Persephone squirms in my grasp. She must realize it too. But she doesn't try to cover herself. She knows better than that. I bite back the urge to praise her for it.

This time, when I lick her, she lets out a wail that's pure embarrassment, mortification. I do it again, and again. She tries to stop me using only the force of her muscles. It's laughably impossible. I will never let her close herself to me. I won't fucking do it. I will lick her in this place until she has no choice but to submit to the fact that I own her.

"Not there," she begs. "Not there, please, you can't—"

I lift my head from her, an act of supreme self-control, and put two fingers where she doesn't want me to go. Persephone writhes, trying to get away, and it is the sweetest torture I've ever known. She's still begging when I push those fingers inside.

She's tight, here. So unbelievably tight. Her begging cuts off into a series of small, pained gasps that have me straining against my own pants. I'll die if I don't fuck her soon.

"Wander off again, and there will be worse punishments than this."

Persephone tenses, mouth open, shadows falling around her face. "Your fingers are too big."

"You'll take them. You deserve them." Something

cracks inside of me and anguish pours out, acrid and cold. "Do you know what you did to me?" I pull my fingers out, bend over her, and kiss her. It's savage enough to draw blood. More pain, deeper pain. I need her to feel it too. She will, and she'll finally fucking understand. "Do you know?"

She couldn't possibly know the depth of what she's done. She couldn't, because there's no way for me to tell her. There's no fucking way to describe the sensation of having your heart ripped out by two small, delicate hands. Admitting it is an arrow between my ribs and a knife in the back. There is nothing more terrible and wounding, but I can't be wounded. I will never allow myself to be wounded.

Except here. Except now.

"Yes," she sobs, her tears glittering in the dim light. "Yes—"

I undo my pants with one hand and shove inside her. I'm half-gone. Merciless. Animal. Whether it's punishment or pleasure makes no difference. Those distinctions are for people, and I am nothing but a raw nerve. She's so fucking perfect, panting and arching and crying. Persephone grips the sides of the desk, trying to stay on. The world narrows until the only thing remaining is her, and the way I'm fucking her, vicious and hard. Like she's property. Like she belongs to me. Because she does. I'm the only man in the world who gets to fuck her until she cries. And I've never loved anything so much in my life.

10

FOR MOST OF MY LIFE, I thought that knowledge would make me feel better. Safer. I tried to get it wherever I could, which wasn't easy. My mother didn't want me to have it. And now I know why.

I don't feel safer.

The world seems enormous, sprawling, dangerous. It seems sharp as it goes by outside the train window and Hades works at his desk. There's so much I didn't know, and everywhere I turn another web is waiting to catch me. In all my plans for escape, I didn't factor in new facts about my mother. Are they even real? They must be. Why would Zeus lie about that? He said those things like they were true. Like he hadn't even considered lying.

I'm parched for more information, the way I've been dying to go and stand by those lions for as long as I've known they existed. It comes with a cost, though, doesn't it? Going to that library isn't free. Knowing things isn't free.

Secrets glitter in the shadows all around us, never quite showing themselves. They've been there all along. Of course they have. It's only now that the curtain's been ripped away.

I was so naive.

Hades didn't appear from nowhere as a full-grown man with cruelty in his hands and pain in his eyes. There was a life. A life. A family. He had one, too. It made him who he is, but I've been imagining him as a dark gash in the middle of the world, independent of everything else. I've been imagining him as the one-dimensional evil that my mother whispered into my ear. She was a liar, too.

My mind struggles to untangle all those lies—all those omissions—all the way back to the mountain. All the way through the soaring rotunda. All the way back to Hades' private wing. I pad along next to him, barefoot and wrapped in a thick blanket from his train car. At the door to the guest suite I turn without thinking.

His hand comes down hard on my shoulder. "No."

It startles me out of the half-dream I've been having. It's very late, or very early, and time seems unstuck from its usual pattern. I blink up at him. "Why?"

"You'll never sleep there again. Walk, or I'll carry you."

He clips off the words, his impatience stinging my skin. Bone-tired. This is what bone-tired means. But when he tugs me toward the double doors at the end of the hall the urge to sleep falls away.

He has never, not once, taken me past those double doors. My teeth chatter gently against one another with the adrenaline rush. I try to tell myself that it's only a bedroom. I fail because it's not. It's not. It's more important than that. I can't express why, not exactly, but when he opens the door and goes through, I hesitate.

I hold my breath.

Hades has done unspeakable things to me. Things I

could never talk about in the light of day. For all he's made me show him, he's never shown me anything. And if I see...

If I see it, there's no going back.

I draw the blanket tighter around my shoulders. The truth is that I want him, and I'm not supposed to. If I close my eyes to what he really is, then at least I can pretend I'm not falling for a monster. That part of me isn't hungry for the cruel things he does. Hungry and wet, even now...

Hades comes back into the hallway, puts a hand on my elbow, and drags me inside. I hear echoes of my own screams from the first day I was here—*I belong to you, I belong to you*—and press my lips tight to keep them from coming out all over again.

He starts to drag me across a sitting room. Of course it's not just a bedroom, of course—

A shout from the hallway stops my heart and the door bursts open again behind us. Hades' grip hardens on my arm and he shoves me behind him. How did they get here? How could they follow us so quickly? I don't want to go back, *please* don't make me go back—

"I'm sorry," someone calls, and I get up the courage to look out from behind Hades. The man who apologized holds the doorframe to keep himself steady while he holds Conor's collar. Conor, who clearly should be sedated in an animal hospital, struggles against the man. Conor, who's alive. He's alive. Bandaged, wounded, but alive. I let out a breath. If he'd died trying to save me, I—I don't know what I would do. "They couldn't keep him in the clinic when the train arrived. I—" He curses, and Conor breaks free from his hand, his nails clicking on the marble tiles.

The dog I thought was a vicious killer comes to us as fast as he can and pushes his nose into the palm of Hades' hand. I tumble to my knees and put my arms around Conor's neck. His body shakes with every wag of his tail and tears sting the corners of my eyes. He tried to save me. He knew that something was wrong with Decker, and he tried to save me. I'm the only one close enough to see the tentative way Hades touches Conor's head, stroking so lightly between his ears.

A heavy silence passes between the two men, so heavy that it gets my attention. The other man is red-haired and stocky with a scar running down

most of his face. He sticks his hands into his pockets, the fabric rough like workmen's clothes, and
looks across at Hades with a frankness that surprises
me. They know each other. He probably knows
Hades better than I do. Is it fear or jealousy that
shivers down the back of my neck? I don't know.

Conor licks the side of my face and nuzzles into my
shoulder. He's a huge dog—big enough to look
normal standing next to Hades—and his affection
pushes me off-balance. It gives me something to
concentrate on other than the breathless tension in
the room and the scar on Oliver's face.

"Persephone, this is Oliver Callahan, my head of
security. Oliver, this is Persephone." Somehow,
Conor manages to lean into Hades' leg and my
body at the same time.

Oliver pulls a hand out of his pocket and gives me a
small wave. "Pleasure to meet you."

"My—my pleasure, too." Good. This is going very
well.

"You'll see him around my rooms," Hades continues. "If I'm not here, he'll deliver my messages."

Why wouldn't you be here? "Okay."

Hades straightens, shifts, and Oliver is his mirror. "Keep everyone out. You know what to do."

"Of course." Oliver disappears through the double doors at a quick pace. Far in the distance I can hear other doors closing. If this were any other time, I'd be terrified of a man who looked like Oliver. The only reason I'm not is because I'm here with Hades. Right—we were about to go into his private space. There will be no more hiding from the truth of him.

And the truth of me.

I bury my face in Conor's shoulder and whisper my thanks to him. I know he's a dog, but it matters. My arms lock around Conor's neck but after a minute he strains gently against me. He wants to follow Hades.

So do I.

I get up and hook my fingers into his collar. Conor tugs me along toward the bedroom, the blanket slipping down over my shoulders. My lips tingle, on the verge of going numb, but Conor—despite his bullet wound—is warm and solid next to me. He's not afraid.

The bedroom door is open.

A massive window, floor-to-ceiling and nearly as high as the ones overlooking his factory, displays the night sky in such perfect detail that it must be fake. Breathtaking, but fake. There's no possible way the stars are so close, so bright. But the stars don't compare at all to the man standing next to a massive bed, all the sheets and blankets the color of midnight. The window gives off enough light for me to see the dips and shadows of his face in profile and not much else. The light from the sitting room falls off behind me and as I step into true dark they switch off completely. The stars get brighter. He gets darker.

Hades went in here ahead of me. He must be expecting me to follow, but it doesn't look that way. He looks alone. Like nobody could ever be watching. He's half-turned away from the door, the muscled lines of his body statuesque and carved from the stars behind him. If he were a statue it would be called Pain. His chest rises so lightly it's hard to see the movement.

It's the hand over his eyes that gives him away.

It steals the last of my breath, and when Conor walks away from me to go to his side I sway on my feet with a lightheaded rush. Conor settles by his side and leans against his leg, insistent. I have a million questions. This is like finally being inside that library in New York City, not just out front but inside, and not being able to touch the books. There's no way to broach the subject of something so personal with my heart in my throat and a dry mouth.

A new need hums into being and wraps itself around those deep instincts for his hands, for his mouth. It's not just the future I need to know about now. It's him. It's all of him. The thought of being inside his mind, with his thoughts, sends a fresh pull of goose bumps over my skin.

He takes his hands away from his eyes and the movement startles me out of awe and into the reality that he means for me to sleep here with him. Here. With him. In his bed.

"Come here."

I go to him without thinking because my lungs feel tight, cutting off the air I need for reason and logic. There's only a starlight anxiety, crisp and clear, in a constellation with no name but that I recognize intimately.

Hades pulls the blanket from my shoulders and

drops it to the floor. Air floods back in, my vision sharpening. I'm ready, I'm ready. Do you know what you did to me? I'm certain that what happened on the train isn't the end of my punishment. I'm certain of it, and I can take it—

"Get into the bed."

For the first time, I hear it—the edge of suffering in his voice. It stops me from asking my usual parade of questions about what's going to happen. It stuns me to hear it. It's as intimate as him pressing his fingers into me while I writhe and beg. More intimate.

It's a scramble to get into the bed, high off the ground, but Hades doesn't seem to notice how awkward and exposing it is to climb this way when I'm completely naked. That urge to ask him what's going on—what's hurting him, really—can only be stifled by holding my breath and wriggling under the covers. They're so soft, light and strong as silk but burnished, like cotton. I'm probably not supposed to be looking but I can't take my eyes off him. Clothes fall in the starlight. His shirt flutters down first, followed by his pants with the clink of his belt buckle. Then he walks around to the other side and gets in. Stretches out.

The starlight dims in a slow fade, easing away with every breath he takes. I discover I'm jiggling my feet, tense and waiting, trying to breathe through the painful closeness of this. How am I supposed to just...fall asleep next to him? Maybe it would be better if I released some of this pressure by just asking a question. I want his voice. I want the truth. I want—

A hand comes down on my thigh, low enough that I take it for what it is—a warning. Stop moving your fucking feet, Persephone.

"Sleep," he says. The last of the light fades away, leaving us in total darkness. I can only feel the sheets, his hand, the rise and fall of him breathing next to me. It's too much to ask. But he's not asking, is he? His touch is a command. And I have no choice but to obey.

11

PERSEPHONE

WHEN MORNING COMES I have to move.

I find myself freed, in a way, and bereft in another way. Hades turned over on his side in the night to the other side of the bed. Sleeping was easier when he made me do it. Now, in the filtered light from the window—I still can't decide if I'm seeing any real light at all—I test the boundaries. I wriggle my toes, then my feet. He doesn't stir. I've never seen him breathe so evenly and deeply and it makes me feel strangely protective of him. As if he could ever need protecting. As if I could ever be the one to give him that. Impossible.

If I was hungry for truth last night, now I'm starving. Ravenous. Deep sleep cleared my head, and this much is obvious: I can't keep living this way. I can't sign contracts and get kidnapped and live in a mountain fortress if I don't understand what's going on. I'm done being a naive child.

And anyway, I know where that road ends up. It ends with days spent in bed, staring uselessly at the wall, heaviness in my chest. The world looks gray when things get that far. It becomes impossible to see beyond the next hour. The next minute.

I'm not going to that place again.

Will I ever go outside again?

I watch the window over Hades' shoulder. It brightens so slowly. No, it must all be illusory. It's an imitation of a real sunrise with all the color stripped out of it. The thought of that kind of sunrise makes my heart ache.

Of all the things from my previous life, I took being outside in summer for granted the most. Wandering through a lush field with a basket in my hand. Feeling new green shoots of grass under bare feet. A flower's stem pulling up from the ground. This life with Hades is carved and polished in a way that's terrible and wonderful, but there will always be a part of me that longs for summer. For blue skies and clouds and flowers in bloom. For wind in the leaves and a breeze in the middle of a hot day. Morning dew. Evening lightning bugs. All of those things.

Maybe I can find a glimpse of it if I look long enough.

Maybe I should start now.

My head is three inches off the pillow at most when the hand glides easily around my throat and pins me back to the bed. The languid morning feeling I had, with all my daydreams about long walks and gardens, is chased away like a shot. Hades looms over me, tracing a path up and down my neck with the pad of his thumb.

"Where do you think you're going?"

The fact of him—tall, unbelievably strong, unbe-lievably dangerous—never gets less shocking. It thrusts me underwater and drags me out again, dripping wet and shivering. Hades is rumpled in a way he never would have let me see before. Has anyone seen him like this before, with a hint of bedhead and one cheek slightly pinker than the other? I reach for his hair and run my fingers through it like I'm not afraid of him. He keeps his grip light on my throat, but he doesn't stop me.

I know what he's capable of, that's why it's hard to answer. I know what I'm inviting. I'm scared of how much I loathe it and how much I want it in equal measure. This—the bed, the bedroom—doesn't feel entirely real. Fear rolls over me again, icy and taunting. All of this could get ripped away any moment.

"I asked you a question." The warning comes with a squeeze. It reminds me that he owns every breath I take.

Another truth: he owned them long before I signed my name above his on a piece of paper. He owned them the first moment I saw them.

"I was going to..." I so desperately want him to touch me, to take me, and at the same time my heart pounds out a warning to go, to run. He's proven himself to relish hurting me. And yet... "I'm tired of so many secrets."

This early in the morning, his eyes are blue. A

skylike, soaring blue shot through with a deeper color like the ocean. And his body over mine throws off heat like a summer day. It lands on my skin and works its way through in a rough, inescapable massage. He has perfect lips. Every time my eyes drop away from his eyes, they land on those lips, those teeth. Every time, it's like seeing him the first time. I work my fingers through his hair and down the side of his face. Hades blinks but doesn't flinch. He stays still, breathing lightly, letting me do it. I feel like a fawn caught in torchlight, but that's an illusion, too. He is completely unconcerned about scaring me. His hand stays at my throat.

"What do you want to know?"

So many things. The hours I spent in Zeus's whorehouse only piled on the questions until they became a rickety stack. But it's hard to breathe when someone so beautiful and mean is so close to me. It would take nothing at all to turn him wild. He already is. He's playing with me.

I gather up every scrap of courage that a trapped animal would have in the hands of a predator and pluck the easiest, simplest questions from the endless well.

"Why do you have windows like this? Weird windows. Why don't you go into the sun? Why do your eyes turn so black? I—I want to know more about you."

"That's three questions and a statement." His eyes trace lazily over my face. My lips. Down lower, to the naked skin underneath his hand. The blanket fell away during the night and I haven't pulled it up, so he can see my peaked nipples and more, if he wants. My body bends for him even when I fight it. I would do it now. I would do anything now.

"Yes." I swallow and he bites his lip. "But you have the answers."

Hades pushes himself up on his elbows, releasing me and caging me in at the same time. When God closes a window he slams the door shut, too. That's the saying, right? Hades hasn't so much as kissed me but I'm turned into fire by the closeness of him. My toes dig into the bed down between his legs and my back arches. It's a fraction of an inch, maybe less, but he sees. Humiliation tightens my chest. I should have known it would mean this. I should have known the cost of getting close to him would be difficult to bear.

He laughs, his voice harsh but still clouded with sleep. "I don't give out information just because a woman begs."

Hades studies me while he says this, eyes dropping lower and lower. What made me this way? What made me so willing to inch my legs apart so that he can take what he wants? What made me so mortified by this fact, so unwilling to do it when he can see? I can't tell if the torture is the fact that he's watching or the fact that I want him to watch.

He looks back into my eyes, and there is no hiding it —he saw. He saw what I was doing, in my stupid, tentative way. I'm dangling from the end of a fishhook. Put me out of my misery. I want to float away on the delicious haze of an orgasm, not stay here, trapped in my own body and struggling to get out.

"I'm not begging," I tell him.

"Exactly."

He starts by rolling one of my nipples between his fingers, as casually as he'd pick up a fork. It lifts me off the bed, my hips rising, eyes fluttering closed. He moves to the other one, this one harsher, more of a pinch. I'm embarrassingly, awfully wet.

"Look at me."

I do look at him, though it makes my cheeks so hot I'm afraid my hair might catch on fire. His command seems to need a response. This is what I wanted—a conversation. If it's going to be a conversation, then I have to keep talking. "If you want me to beg, I'll beg."

He lowers his mouth to my breast and bites, then repeats it on the other side. He's so slow and deliberate and awful. The only sign he feels any of this is an increased tension in his biceps. He wants to let himself fall, doesn't he? He wants to let himself crush me. Fuck me. But he won't do it. Hades is an expert at holding back. Which will mean...

"I always want you to beg," he says lightly, eyes back on my face. I wish I could stop panting, get a full breath, but I can't. "We've discussed this. I want you to beg, and scream, and cry."

"Then—"

"Make you?"

A hand on my jaw, his lips on mine, rough and cold. I can't breathe, I can't breathe. I don't want to breathe in anything but him. His other hand is everywhere, but nowhere it needs to be. He shoves my legs into a wide-open position, wide enough to accommodate his hips, and works himself between my knees. But he won't touch me.

He once called me a twisted little slut, and he was right.

It breaks over me in a wave, my twisted slut desire. I've been holding it at bay. Keeping it separate from me, because what does it make me if I really am a twisted slut for Luther Hades? I've always been good. I've been so good. I've only ever told lies meant to preserve my safety. I never wanted to hurt anyone else. I especially didn't want to hurt my mother. The cards on that table, long ago, flicker back into my mind in this moment. The cards predicted this, all of this, and I'm doing it anyway. The world has been destroyed twice now, and I'm in his bed, rocking my hips toward him, kissing him back.

I try to pull his face in closer, try to bring us together, but he shoves my hands away with a ruthless strength. He pins them above my head. He won't let me get closer. My hips meet empty air. He's so close—it would only be a matter of inches. My pussy aches for him, my clit starved for pleasure, and if he doesn't touch me or let me touch him I'll die.

I will actually die.

Hades doesn't seem to care. He pushes my hands against his headboard and keeps them there, his other arm balancing him just out of my reach. I think of crawling on the floor to him. I think of his fingers between my legs on his balcony. I think of the way he took me the first time, how much it hurt, how much I wanted it—how I knew he wouldn't stop until he was finished. That's what I want from him now. That's what I need from him now and he is refusing me, he's...

He's laughing at me.

He's delighting in this, in my frustration and desperation.

Fury rises into a scream that I let loose into his mouth, then yank my head away. "Are you happy now? You did it." God help me, I can't stop thrusting my hips. I cannot stop searching for him. I can't stop wanting. I am his twisted little slut. "You made me scream..." The words become another cry.

The hand on my jaw turns my head back toward his. Hades' eyes blaze. He's proud of himself. I pull against his hand and get absolutely nowhere. "Am I happy?" He throws the words at me like tiny daggers. "No, Persephone. I'm not. If you want my secrets, you'll pay the price."

12

I'M SO ANGRY, so hungry. I *do* want his secrets. I'm already paying the price of daring to want more than my mother's fields. I can pay more. But it's not rational, this want that takes me over. It's in my muscles and bones and the hot flush of my face. Anger burns through me and fear chases along with it and the mix is so intoxicating I don't know if I'll ever get over it.

"I'll pay it." I get the words out through gritted teeth. "You name the price and I'll pay it. I—I'll trade."

"What's your counter-offer?"

My counteroffer is that he should do whatever he's

going to do, he should hurt me, he should pleasure me—all of it. He should do anything other than frustrate me like this. The things he's done have been bad enough. They've turned me into a twisted little slut. The phrase rings in my ears. *Never is a long time* rings in my ears. He's so cold and businesslike, as if we're discussing an addendum to the contract we signed.

My hips meet air again and again while he watches with detached amusement. I'm a writhing mess. I am nothing. He's everything. I love it and I hate it and I need it.

What's left for me to give to him? I already belong to him. I already said that, cried it, screamed it. His people have been between my legs and everywhere else, preparing my body for him. He has invaded every possible part of me. What else can I offer? Anxiety tips itself into my mind and freezes me in place. What can I say? *What can I say?*

He watches my struggle with cold interest for another beat. "Ah. It looks like you need to be taught a lesson about hesitation."

"No—"

No is the only word that affects him. Hades yanks me up off the bed until our faces are almost touching. "Yes."

Then he's moving, so fast I can't anticipate him, so confident I can't keep up. Hades drags me off the bed and pushes me to my knees on the floor. He strokes my hair back from my face, leaving no strand to distract me. It takes my breath away, how gentle it is. It takes the next breath, too, because it must be some kind of trap, some kind of trick. He would never be gentle. The image of him standing there, hand against his eyes, comes back to me. Maybe he would be gentle. Maybe that's in him somewhere, along with the ability to feel pain.

"Open your mouth."

I hesitate again. Not because I don't want to obey him but because I do. What will be left of me if he consumes me completely?

It's too late.

He only needs one hand to force my jaw open. He uses the other to show me how hard he is, how huge. These are things I will never stop learning. I will always be shocked. I'm shocked now, trembling on my knees on carpet so plush it reminds me of untouched grass. The air in the room slides between my parted thighs and strokes me where I wish he would.

His free hand comes back to my face and for once it's a light touch. A thumb brushing over my cheek-bone. Fingertips skimming over my lips. Like he's memorizing me, though I can't imagine what he'd need to do that for. I'll be with him forever.

Hades tests my teeth with the pad of his thumb and coaxes my mouth open wider. "I'm going to fuck your mouth now, Persephone. I've waited long enough."

Take it, take it. Accept it, and you'll have a chance at getting what you want.

"I can't," I blurt out. "It's too big." His cock bobs in front of my face and I'm so torn. I can't look away from it. But I need to look at him, because what's the point of begging otherwise? All the bravery I've built up—and it's not much—flees. My lip quivers. I'm not going to cry over this, damn it. I want this. I want to be here, on my knees before a king. That's what he is. He rules everything in sight and out of sight, including me.

"It will choke me," I whisper.

He makes me look up into his eyes. "Yes, it fucking will."

Hades puts a hand on the back of my head to steady me and I get a final burst of courage. "What do I get? Will you answer my questions?"

He tips his head back and laughs. "You'll get what I give you. All of it."

Hades silences my last-gasp attempt at an argument with the full length of him. It shouldn't be a shock at this point. I should not be surprised. The night he took me for the first time I thought that he could never feel bigger than when he was splitting me apart. Everything I think turns out to be so, so wrong.

Except for the choking. I was right about the choking. It happens almost immediately because Hades isn't kind or gentle or any of the things I'd expect from another man. He's himself. He promised he would fuck my throat. He's following through. I gag on him, and no amount of self-control can keep my hands down by my sides. The skin of his thighs turns pink under the sharp moons of my nails.

Hades groans.

He works his fingers through my hair and holds me in place, tugging at intervals to keep me close. Tears gather and spill down onto my breasts, all down the front of me.

"Yes," he says, almost to himself. His fingers swipe at the tears and I swear I hear him lick them off his fingers.

Hades pulls out long enough for me to gasp in a breath. There is no other reprieve and I don't expect one. The shocks come one after the other in a relentless roll. Thrust. Gasp. Breathe. Try to keep my head above water. Cry around the hard length of him. Another thrust. Another gasp.

It's not long, or maybe it's hours later, that his rhythm breaks down. His fists curl tight in my hair and I flatten my tongue, trying to give him room. There's no more room to take. He holds tighter. Begging with your mouth full is a wordless, shameful experience. It pushes Hades right to the edge. He loses all sense of his strokes and shoves in deep. He's going to kill me and the darkest, dirtiest part of me is going to love it.

"Fuck, Persephone. Hold still."

I have to hold still. I can't go anywhere else. My toes are already braced into the carpet and if I hold his thighs any tighter I'll draw blood. Air—air. I need air. Instead I get the hot spill of his release. There's so much to swallow, so much, oh my god. A dark cloud pushes in at the edges of my vision and I can't tell if it's because I'm dying or because I'm dying for him.

He pulls away and I fall forward onto my hands and knees. I'd crawl for him right now. I'd do it, if he would touch me. I would do anything. But he casually steps around behind me and lifts me in his arms. Hades carries my gasping, glassy self to the wide sill set into the window. I wait for him to bend me over it, for this to escalate into something that will leave me sleeping off an orgasm for several hours, but instead Hades pins me to himself and hits some hidden switch.

The window becomes an actual window. It's green out there. His arm glides around my neck. Anywhere else, I'd be his hostage. But here? I don't know what I am. Except for his. There is an actual valley outside the window and a small part of me aches to be out there almost as much as I want to be in here with him.

"What is that place?" I whisper. More details come into focus. A small house at the edge of all the green. Tiny white flowers. A small figure in the distance. This place should be impossible. It shouldn't exist.

"You were a good girl." The compliment makes me want to melt into him, despite everything, despite the way it's meant to cut me. "You've earned the answer to one question. Are you sure you want it to be what is this place?"

I buy myself a beat with a long inhale.

"Choose quickly. Or I can teach you some more about the consequences of hesitation. I'll gladly accept your payment a second time."

I can't do it. There's no way I can do it. My throat feels bruised and I'm unsteady on my feet. A light-headed mess. I can't do it, but I will if that's what it takes. The space between my legs is molten and raw and he hasn't even touched me. He won't touch me. I need him to touch me.

The window, the valley, his hand tantalizingly close to my clit but not quite there, not where I need it. The obvious thing to ask him about is the window.

The dark room. The mountain. The way he was standing last night. Does it hurt you?

"Zeus."

He holds me tighter. "That's not a question."

"He said—he said—" I fight for a semblance of control over myself but I don't have it. I want to be outside. I want to be bent over this windowsill. I want to be back in his bed. "He said you're his brother. That you and my mother are siblings." Hades shifts his weight to one side, then the other, and the angle of the window makes it feel like I could fall straight through it to the valley below. Would he save me? "Is it true?"

Now his hand goes in the wrong direction. I could cry. He'd probably like it. But I've already cried so much, and gagged so much, that I'm not sure I have the energy. "The same man adopted the three of us."

I sag into his arm, the most depraved, disgusting possibility vaporating. A tiny part of all this makes slightly more sense—mainly the way that he and Zeus look nothing alike. Nothing alike at all. And neither of them look like my mother. I could never have guessed. The future where that betrayal happens veers away and disappears.

Hades scrapes a nail along each of my ribs, teasing me, taunting me. His hand moves down only an inch at a time.

"My relationship with Zeus and Demeter is a technicality." His voice is a low rumble in my skin. It goes all the way through to my heart. His fingers sink lower and lower and my hips try to find him again. The wanting will never end. I'll be doing this forever. I grit my teeth to keep from begging any more. "Here's a small reward, since you let me fuck your mouth until you cried. Are you ready?"

"Yes. I am, I am—"

Please, let the reward be a chance to come. Let it be that, because if it's not I won't survive this. Let it be that, because I will never relax again for the rest of my life if he leaves me like this. I'm wound up so tight that only someone else's hands can free me. Only his hands. And another possible future dies— the future where I could tolerate anyone else. It's a distant door closing down and becoming part of the wall, like it never existed. It's a shadow ship where everything is the same, only I never feel like this again. I hate feeling like this. I'm sure I do.

He leans down and his fingers finally make contact. One final shuddering sob escapes me. "I hate them both," Hades says into my ear, his voice calm and measured, the opposite of the fever dream I'm currently living. "Just like real siblings."

13

THE LAST WORD floats out of his mouth and he drops me.

He *drops* me.

Hades lets go, stepping back, and I catch myself on the windowsill. A reflection of the room comes into focus. The bed. The scattered clothes. Hades, rubbing a hand over his mouth.

"Stay," I say to his reflection. Is it me, or does he hesitate?

Hades drops his hand and straightens. "It would be too much."

By the time I whirl around to demand an explanation he's gone. Somewhere down a short hallway a door closes. Water starts running a minute later. Too much? What could he have meant by that? Hades has never cared about what's too much for me. Unless he means to drag this out a little longer, play with me some more...

I crawl back into the bed and pull the sheet up. The sound of the water blocks out everything else. He could have taken me into the shower with him. It would have been kinder. Sexier, anyway. I muffle my laugh with the pillow. This is what I wanted. I wanted to buy his secrets from him, and this is part of the price.

Fine. He can lock me out here, away from him, and I can do what I want.

I follow the path of his hand with my own fingers and squeeze my eyes closed. He fills my mind like he's there in bed with me. The only impressions that matter are his hands on my skin and his cock filling me. The small release I get doesn't compare to what I might have had if he'd given it to me, but it's enough. It's enough to let me breathe but not enough to settle my racing heart. I'm not going to be the person who follows him into the shower. Not today.

I throw back the covers and go to the hallway, where I find another door that leads to a walk-in closet three times the size of the one in the guest suite. This one is all man—all pressed suits and sharp shirts, a neat row of polished shoes. All of it smells like him.

All of it except the new row of clothing, which is mine.

I recognize it from before I left. There's my red caftan. This feels like home. But not the home I shared with my mother. A new home, somewhere in that hazy future. And now that I'm dressed, I need to get a grip on myself.

The small library is just as I left it. Not a speck of dust out of place. Hades' people have been through here cleaning, the way they always do. The world here didn't stop because I was gone. But the real comfort is taking a book from the shelves and curling up in the chair with it. No fire necessary. The temperature in here has been adjusted so I don't need more than the caftan and I'm not overheated.

The book is a filthy romance.

It's explicit, raunchy, the kind my mother would

never let me read. It has diamonds and gold on the cover, and I sink into it like I sank into Hades' bed. Nervously. Tentatively. Finally my head detaches from the world and I lose myself in this story of a rich man in love with his own secretary.

By the time I manage to put it down and go back to Hades' room, he and Conor are gone.

So it's my turn to get ready for the day. It should be a simple act, showering and dressing, and it is. But it's not my simple act. This is not how I've gotten ready every day of my life, but it doesn't feel as strange as it should. Standing on the big black tiles in Hades' bathroom should have me quaking in fear, but I'm not. Choosing another dress from my space in his closet should have my heart beating so hard it gives out, but my pulse only races and thrills. How did this place begin to feel like mine? It's not mine. But maybe all those linen dresses and fields weren't mine, either.

A soft knock at the door scares the shit out of me. I wrench my hand away from the shirt of Hades' I've been touching. I wasn't thinking.

It's Oliver, the redheaded man with the scar on his face. Hades' head of security.

He clears his throat. "Mr. Hades wanted you to know that he'll be back this evening."

He hovers in the entryway of the closet.

"What aren't you saying, Oliver?"

A half-smile makes the scar stand out even more, but it also gives a new depth to Oliver's eyes. "He'd like you to stay in his private wing. If he wishes to see you, he'll send word to me and I'll bring you to his office."

I trace a finger around one of the buttons on the shirt. "Right. Because I'm his prisoner."

"It's for safety's sake," Oliver says. "I'll be at the main entrance to his quarters all day if you need anything."

Oliver goes to stand guard and I'm left alone in all the empty rooms. I go back to the book in the library, but it doesn't hold my attention as well as this puzzle does. Oliver didn't deny that I'm Hades' prisoner, but there's more to it than that. Or am I just imagining things—getting it wrong, the way I always do? No. I heard his voice in the train car and this morning in his rooms. There's more. For both of us.

But Hades is the only one who gets to disappear into his office while I stay here, a princess in a tower.

I put the book on the nightstand and wander from room to room. The sitting room. The bedroom. The entryway, with its sunken living room. The kitchen. The guest suite. I discover a small gym with a hot tub attached.

I'm definitely his prisoner. I signed up to be his prisoner. I traded my life away, and now I'm in the middle of a series of deals with the most dangerous man in the world.

After an hour, a woman appears to tidy Hades' bedroom, and leaves with a nod of her head like she's stepped out of the past. Another hour ticks by. The silence starts to get to me. I sing a few songs I remember from childhood and lapse back into the quiet of my thoughts.

Hades left me in here. He left me frustrated and needy, and there's only one other thing I want as much as I want him to come back—I want more. More facts. More knowledge. More explanations for the tangled web that is my life, both before him and with him now. On my next loop through his private wing I stop outside the closed door to his office.

My mouth goes dry, a familiar fear setting in. If Oliver catches me, he'll tell Hades. Then again, if I spend the rest of my days doing nothing except wearing a path in the carpet, I'll never make it. The risk makes me feel...alive.

I'll try the door. That's all. If it's locked, I'll give up. If it's locked it wasn't meant to be. I put one finger on the smooth handle.

That's all it takes for the door to swing open.

It's not locked.

14

PERSEPHONE

I'VE BEEN HERE BEFORE, more than once, but never alone. Never like this. I feel rushed, like there's not enough time, but there is. He won't be back soon.

Hades' office, like everywhere else, was made for him. That makes all the furniture—his desk and two chairs across from it, and the overstuffed chair by the fireplace—too large for me. One of the books my mother approved was Through the Looking Glass. In this moment I'm Alice, but there's no magic tea cake that will make me fit into this world.

I'll fit myself in, then.

But first I listen for any sign that Oliver's back in here. There is none.

This part is easy. If Oliver appears, I can say that I was only exploring. That I was revisiting the site of my contract signing. That I was doing almost anything but snooping.

The next part isn't so innocent.

Well, fine. I'm not innocent. I'm not the girl in white linen who came here with Hades on the train. That girl is gone now. It's a new person who steps behind Hades desk and bends low to try his drawers.

My pulse thrums in my ears. Not now, anxiety, this is important work. My nerves don't cooperate. Why should they? They're trying to warn me that this is reckless, this is dangerous, that any number of things could happen to me from taking this chance. Any number of things have already happened to me. That's my answer to my stupid feelings. I need more of those things to happen.

In the narrow top drawer, I find an empty pill bottle. I roll it curiously in my palm. There's no label on it, so it could belong to anyone. But it doesn't—it belongs to Hades. I don't need to second-guess that. What was in the pill bottle is another story. He'd make me pay for it. I don't know how much more payment I can take today.

I put the bottle back.

The second drawer down is locked.

The third door pops open to reveal...

Files.

Lots of files in a neat, thick row. This is the kind of thing my mother used to have in her filing cabinet. She kept her files under lock and key and she kept the key under her pillow. I was never allowed to know what was in those cabinets, on those papers. Maybe that's why I sink my hands down into them so I can feel the heft. There is so much here to know. My fingernails make a zipping sound along the top of the files. It's business documents, not personal things, but I could sit here and read them all day. Hades has read them. If I did too, we'd finally have a similarity between us.

An off-white page at the bottom of the cabinet catches my eye in the middle of separating the folders from one another so I can peek inside. I shove them farther apart. There's not much extra room—too many documents—but I manage to reveal more of the paper.

The logo at the very top makes my breath catch.

It's my mother's logo.

From what I know of the world—and I know it's not much—it wouldn't be that unusual to have a business deal with someone you hated. This deal, though—this is an old deal. I know, because the logo is old. It's five or six versions ago. The last time my mother used that logo on her envelopes and letterhead, I was three. Maybe four.

I try to convince myself it's not that weird. If Zeus, Hades, and my mother were all adopted by the same person, then they knew each other before this logo was made. I'm probably not looking at anything that matters. Zeus even said something about this—how my mother uses Hades in the same way Zeus does. What did he mean? I wish I'd been less of a coward.

I can be less of a coward now.

The paper won't tell me anything new. I'm sure of it. That's why I'm just going to read it quickly, then put it back before anyone notices I'm here. I use one hand to brace the files. For a man with a meticulous closet, he's got too many things in this drawer. If I'm not going to wrinkle the page at the bottom beyond all recognition, I'll have to do this very slowly. My hand goes down first and the files neatly pin my wrist between them. I'm almost there, almost there...

My fingertips brush the corner of the paper. It's thick paper, but old, and the texture reminds me of my mother's phase when she sold paper products, too. Did she make this? I'm dying to know.

A movement at the door, movement in the air.

"What are you doing?"

15

PERSEPHONE IS adorable when she's caught red-handed. I will never get tired of the way the way she gasps, startled. She assumes that she won't get caught. That's what's so striking. I can see in her face that she genuinely assumed I wouldn't be here. That I could stay away until the evening. It hasn't been four hours.

She squirms away from the filing cabinet and kicks it shut, her cheeks red, biting her lip. If it wasn't this cabinet, of all the fucking filing cabinets, I might let it go.

No. I wouldn't. I like it too much when she cries. And I like how hard she comes afterward.

I try to ignore the tick of my pulse at the side of my neck. She's been here less than a day, and already she's come dangerously close of discovering the one secret I won't let her buy. That secret is fucking priceless, like the location of a live atom bomb. To find her like this, about to set it off—

The sight of her in a blue dress she found in my closet overwhelms me. Inflames me. Earlier today I decided to exercise some self-restraint with her. Now that I have her back, I need to pace myself. I can't devour her in a single day. I can't hurt her. Not like that.

There are other ways I can hurt her. Other ways I will hurt her. Getting close to her, even for this, is like stepping into a hot room in winter. My skin is supersensitive to my clothes. It has been since I put them on this morning, but now the sensation is intensified a hundredfold. My hands ache to touch her, but that's only superficial—it's an ache that extends to the parts of me I can't let her see. The only way to sate myself is to make that pain her only reality.

What I can't do is let her know how precarious this little game is. For me, not her. While she babbles an apology, I swallow the stupid, harmful urge to tell her everything. I've never been so reckless and I won't start now. Fuck that. I know how vulnerability ends. It ends with listening to the things you love struggle for a final breath in the hands of a person you hate. I'll fucking play, because she wants to— because her eyes get so wide and hopeful, because her body loves being bent and punished. But I can only give her scraps at a time. My better instincts will prevail.

My better instincts need her now.

From the way she looks guiltily down at the filing cabinet and tries not to keep her hands in sight, I know she's done more than search around in a document cabinet. Persephone can wear blue and red and pretend she's not that linen-clad little thing, fresh off her mother's fields, a new flower waiting to be plucked. But she is. We have much further to go before she turns into an autumn bloom.

I go to her and she doesn't run, she only trembles like the angel of air and sunlight that she is. She knows there is no escape from this darkness. She knows, and she still tries.

"I got carried away," she says urgently as I bend her over the desk with a hard shove that doesn't leave room for argument. Persephone finds the crack in the wall. One errant tear flees down her cheek. Don't worry, sweetheart. There will be more. "I wasn't—I wasn't trying to get into your business."

I take a fistful of her hair, digging in until she whimpers.

Fuck. I thought I'd killed and buried all these feelings, the hurt and the fear and the sick, pointless jealousy. Persephone is a conduit for those feelings. They radiate from her, drawing them out of wherever they'd gone to hide. I fucking hate that. She can never discover how helpless I am to her—to the need to come back to her, over and over again. Perhaps she already knows, and that's why she's chosen this as a way to entertain herself while she belongs to me. Forever is a long fucking time. If she puts her mind to it, she'll buy every last secret from me. Except the one that's not for sale.

"Here is what you may know about my business." I take a pen from the drawer closest to her and slam it shut, which causes a cascade of movements—she jumps, pulling harder against my hand, and lets out another half-cry. I wanted to fuck her long before I stepped into this room and now I want it so much that my practiced denial is crumbling under an onslaught of feverish need. "Are you paying attention?"

Persephone's eyes flick up toward me. With my fist in her hair and her head turned to the side, she has no choice but to pay attention. I just want to see those tears in her eyes. Her mouth forms the word yes.

I draw an x on the calendar page that takes up most of the desk. As a rule, I never keep appointments on it. It's only there so I can mark the passage of time. Every day gone is one less day I don't have to live with myself.

"This is my business." A few inches below the X, I scrawl a rectangle. "This is your mother's operation."

"Wedding flowers," Persephone whispers.

"Drugs."

Persephone stiffens. "No, she—she makes bouquets for people."

Demeter kept her daughter prisoner for years. I know she wasn't kind—Demeter hasn't been kind for years, despite the earth mother bullshit she uses as a front for her brand. She has her reasons. I study Persephone, the quiver in her chin and the way she worries at her lip. It carves out a space in my chest. One I can't bear. She'll go to the ends of the earth to defend her mother. I know, because once upon a time I would have done the same for my father. It took me years to grow out of that tortured, misguided longing.

"No, sweetheart, she doesn't." Persephone flinches at *sweetheart*. Good. Below the rectangle I draw a bigger box. "And here is Zeus's whorehouse. He had you dressed up as one of them. Any guesses what he planned to do?"

She shakes her head. For a moment I consider making her guess. It would turn her on. Persephone is already wet. I don't have to reach beneath her skirt to know it.

Around all three marks I draw a circle, then throw the pen into the corner of the room. It hits the wall and clatters down. With infinite restraint I move Persephone's head over the collection of marks and stab a finger onto the paper. "Be a good girl and tell me what the circle is."

"The train." She tries to get up, but only succeeds in arching her back in a way that is going to take me out at the knees. "It's the train."

"What else?"

"I don't know." She can't get my hand out of her hair and more than that she's rocking back toward me. A greedy little slut. I push her all the way flat on the desk. Persephone barely turns her head in time to avoid getting her nose in the ink from my pen. My most fervent wish is that I could fuck her right now, like this, but there are punishments to be metered out first. She can't get into the habit of digging in my cabinets.

I lean down next to her ear. "Money. Drugs and whores are frowned upon by the federal government. They need my diamonds to make their money legitimate." It pains me to stand up, but I do it anyway. "Our father was a titan of illegal businesses. Once he was gone, it made sense for Zeus and Demeter to take over what they could."

I let go of Persephone's hair because I need both hands free and because if I keep fucking talking, I'll tell her too much. Demeter has truly hidden every-thing from her, that bitch. She should have given her a basic lesson about how her life works. Now she'll come to a far more painful understanding. At least I get to enjoy it.

"What happened to him?"

"We ate him alive."

I take her wrists and pull her forward so that her hands are off the other side of the desk, then pick up a small glass statue that normally sits at the corner of my desk. For years, it's been a reminder of an unfulfilled contract. I turn Persephone's hands palm up and make her hold it. Her fingers explore the shape.

"A poppy?" she whispers.

I ignore this. We're not getting into the details of my agreements now. Not when I've already destroyed what little peace was left between Zeus and I. The repercussions of that fucking poppy go far beyond our financial ties.

"I know I shouldn't have looked," Persephone says to the poppy. Is she just now realizing the conse-quences she's brought on herself? "I just thought—"

"It's too late for that now."

I step back behind her and the sun catches in the paperweight. It shouldn't be possible because of the windows, but the fucking sun has sought out the perfect angle to refract into my eyes, a stab straight through the head. It causes a brief loss of control in the form of a curse under my breath. I unbuckle my belt and slide it through the loops, test it in my hand. I shove the skirt of her dress up to her waist. She's naked underneath.

Persephone looks back toward me the best she can.

"Is it the light that hurts you?"

"Yes." Fuck. I'm not thinking anymore, with heated blood and a pounding heart, and I need to fucking think. No. I need to hurt. I need to have. Slipping up like that is not an option. "But my belt will hurt you more. Ten if you can obey. Twenty if you drop the glass."

I bring it down onto her skin and she howls, throwing her head back, but she keeps the statute in her hand and stays still. The stripes are so red and she sound of her cries is so cleansing. It focuses my mind. It's a release and a torture at the same time, because—two more—it's not enough to claim her with leather. I want flesh, too. Need it.

Four. Five. Six.

"You're here in my private quarters because I need you." Another fucking slip. I meant to say I need to protect you. I can't fucking stop myself. "Don't fuck this up, sweetheart. Don't disobey me."

Seven. Eight. Nine.

She's crying, tears flooding down her cheeks, face red. The sound of it hooks into my hidden places and drags me toward her. I lean down close. This next part she needs to hear, even though she's sobbing. Especially because she's sobbing. And because I need another opportunity to breathe her in, to put my lips close to her skin.

"Don't go looking through my desk."

I drive the last point home with a final strike. Persephone screams, her knees buckling, but she holds onto that damn paperweight like it's a lifeline. The belt falls to the floor first, and I follow it to my knees. Force her legs apart. Drink her in.

She is wet. I was right. And she tastes so fucking

sweet that an old springtime explodes in my mouth. A clear day, my first dog still alive by my side, before summer was a killing pain. One breath—that's all it takes for her screams to turn to moans.

16

PERSEPHONE

I'M NOTHING BUT THROBBING, heated flesh and this delicate poppy statue. Nothing, nothing. His punishment has left me a blank slate. Everything is chased away from my mind except the bruising pain on my ass and the slick, hot pleasure between my legs. If I didn't know better I'd think I was drunk. That's how it feels with Hades hands between the desk and my hips, pulling me back to his mouth. That's how it feels, staring into the light captured in the statue. He—he didn't say when I could put it down, so I'm going to assume that the answer is never. I'll hold onto this statute for the rest of my life if he keeps doing what he's doing.

It feels so good. Not the crack of his belt—that felt bad, very bad. But every single stroke drove my desire deeper between my legs. He knew I was ready for him. I heard the sound he made when he knelt down behind me. I heard it, unless it's part of a grand hallucination I'm having. The statue is what grounds me. It was real before this started, and it's real now, so the rest of it must be real.

My hips have nowhere to go. Hades told me to stay still, didn't he? If he didn't he's making it happen through the force of his will and the hard boundary of the desk. There's nowhere to go, so I open myself to him. He wants more than that. His fingers dig in and spread. I can't hide anything, I can't— and I don't want to. All I want is to come.

His tongue takes me there. The rhythm is too fast —*wait*, I try to scream, but nothing comes out except an anguished moan. His answer is another series of punishing licks. I'm getting hauled toward a vicious orgasm by a machine of a man. Crying makes no difference to him. It's unbearably sexy.

My orgasm winds and winds until it finally snaps, so powerful that I'm begging for him to stop almost as soon as it starts. He doesn't stop. He keeps going and going until he's devoured it from me, until I'm hanging limp over the desk. Still holding onto the glass poppy. I won't let go. I won't earn myself another ten strokes with his belt. I won't, I won't.

He stands up behind me and one hand comes down on the desk, then the other. Thank you, desk. Without you I'd be a limp mess on the floor. Without you I wouldn't be standing. The hard crown of him demands entrance and Hades takes me with one hard thrust of his hips.

This time, I'm not the only one breathing hard.

He's a wild thing, all his muscle and power concentrated into fucking me. It forces the air from my lungs every time he enters. Hold onto the poppy, hold on, hold on. My ass smarts from the extra contact. Oh, it hurts, it hurts, I need it to hurt. A bolt of anger goes through me—why punish me like this? Why make me hold this stupid statue when I could be scrabbling at the desk and digging my nails into him? Because it's better this way. Because I like it better this way. Twisted. Terrible. Dark.

Light. Caught in glass, where I wouldn't expect it to stay, but it does.

Thoughts come one by one into my mind.

All of this is connected.

The poppy.

The papers.

The man behind me, driving into me with complete abandon.

Pleasure and heat locking themselves together between my legs, skimming over a layer of pain that heightens everything until another orgasm sneaks up and pulls me under. Far under. One time when I was very small my mother took me to the beach. I didn't see the wave until it was on top of me. Has Hades ever seen what water looks like from below the surface, with salt stinging his eyes and his lungs fighting for air? Has he ever felt that shock? He's like a dark, unfamiliar room. None of our experiences line up.

Except this one.

This one...

Now.

He says something I don't hear because all of my energy is focused on his cock inside me and the statue balanced on my palms. If I hold it as tight as he's holding me I'll break it. That will be enough for him to punish me. Of course it would. This is a precious object.

Then he pushes himself inside, so deep it makes me cry out again—I will never stop, never stop—and his superheated release paints my insides.

"Fuck," he says. "Fuck." His hands tighten on my hips, making me stay frozen to the desk. For once he's the one with aftershocks rolling through him. I can feel them everywhere. My face flushes—he just fucked me over a desk and I'm the one blushing. Why?

Hades banishes the thought with a final sharp slap to my ass, which layers itself on top of the burn and sinks in deeper. A shadow falls over me. I brace for more, fleetingly think of begging for it, but he only plucks the statue from my hands and puts it back on the desk.

It was the statue holding me up, then. I slide off the surface of his desk unceremoniously, landing heavily in his arms before I hit the carpet. No, I'm going to tell him. I can walk. But I can't.

Hades carries me somewhere else. Light and shadow go by as he walks. I only know we're back in the bedroom when he tips me into the sheets.

The window's gone dark again but I curl up on my side and look toward it anyway. Hades stands at the edge of the bed. It's not like him, to take so long to decide. I'm already drifting off, letting go of the aches in my body and my heart, when the mattress bends. It's another long while before he runs his fingers through my hair. It's not easy, with hair like mine. You have to work at it. Maybe he can only be this gentle when I'm not looking at him.

"I've said too much," he mentions absently a while later. "You do that to me."

My mouth doesn't want to work, but if he's inviting me to have a conversation, then we will have a conversation. "Do what?"

He sighs. "Make me lose control of myself."

I think it through, my mind hazy from whatever that was. Punishment. Pleasure. Both. "We could make another trade."

His fingertips come down on my naked hip, and then he pulls the blanket up over me. "I already own you. What else could you give?"

"I've thought about it." Wake up, wake up. Stay

awake. "The only thing you don't have are my new thoughts. What's inside my head right now."

"What gives you the idea that I care what you're thinking about?"

"You're still here," I whisper. "So you must want something else. And you can take anything you want from me. You can extract payment. You're so big and strong, I can't stop you." I press my thighs together. It does nothing to stamp out the new shoots of desire there. "All I have are new thoughts."

"That's ridiculous." He's silent for a long time. "Give them to me."

I'm on the edge of drifting off, but I haul myself hand over hand back to enough of a semblance of consciousness that I can talk to him. "I used to dream about buildings. The New York Public Library." The taste of the words is so familiar. An old dream. "I used to dream of walking by the lions out front on forty-second street." I was never allowed to go to anywhere large enough to have a forty-second street. He's never going to let me go, either. That's why it's a dream. A fantasy. It doesn't compare to his fingers in my hair. "Going inside. There are so many books there."

"I gave you a library stuffed with books, you ungrateful little brat." There's no sting behind the words.

"So?" I say, like an ungrateful little brat. "I wanted to go to the New York Public Library. That's where I've always wanted to go." I can't open my eyes—my eyelids are far too heavy for that—but his body next to mine spurs me on. "Anyway, I was talking about my dreams. I dreamed of that place. I used to dream about it all the time. I would be there without my mother, and nobody would be able to stop me from reading anything I wanted. I've seen pictures. It's beautiful there."

"What do you dream of now?"

My eyes fill with tears behind my eyelids. I let one or two escape. My throat tightens but I swallow it back. I'm not going to cry over this. If I cry, it will be because I'm wrung out and ragged after this morning and being taken over Hades' desk. I get full control of myself before I answer him.

"Being outside." That was my last burst of energy. I tumble down into sleep. Hades' hand slows in my hair. I don't care if he's watching me now. I can't help it. His hand is still, a calming warmth. "I really like to be outside."

"Picking flowers in your mother's fields." He sounds so far away. Stay. I need to stay and ask him what he means, but it's too late.

17

PERSEPHONE

I DIDN'T LIE. I dream of being outside, someplace wide-open and warm. Bare feet on new grass. A basket in my hand. There's no boundary marked by trees, so I can see for miles. It's miles and miles of wildflowers. Rare flowers. I can fill my basket. I could walk for hours. On the next step, the sole of my foot meets something shiny and flat. Way out here, in the middle of nowhere? I lift my foot away from it like it's a land mine, holding my breath.

It's not a mine, it's a card. A tarot card. I recognize it from all those years ago—the purple and black pattern on the back of the cards. This one has a small tear in the corner. Dream-logic compels me to bend down and pick it up. Sweat breaks out on the back of my neck. If I don't look, then I won't have to see which card it is. But I already know.

Death.

I flip it over in my hand—there's that skull, that darkness. "Death," a voice says. A presence lurks behind me but when I turn, nobody's there. The card sticks to my fingers when I try to let it fall. It reminds me of a mayfly. It has wings, like a mayfly. It won't get off, *it won't get off*—

I wake up with a muffled shriek, fighting with the blankets in Hades' bedroom. He was here when I went to sleep but he's not here now. The window offers zero clue as to what time it is, but judging by the sleepiness clinging to my bones, it's been a long time since I fell asleep. Maybe the rest of the afternoon and night. That seems right. I'm still in the same clothes as....before. The ache in my ass has subsided, but it's not gone. The next day. I've lost an afternoon and a night with Hades.

Or maybe without him. I don't know where he went. On the way out of the Ed a glimmer catches my eye. A piece of jewelry, high on his pillow. A gift.

I hold my breath while I pick it up. A bracelet. Diamonds in a silver thread, like he took the sky and made it small enough to hang around my wrist. Is he watching? No, but my face flushes and I put it on quickly before I get caught. Doing what, I don't know. Having a crush, maybe. Embarrassing.

Showering would be a good first step, but before that I pad out into the sitting area to make sure he's really gone.

Hades is.

Oliver isn't.

He's bent over a newspaper when I step through the door and he startles, dropping his pen. What was he doing with the pen, annotating the newspaper? Seems weird. But then again, Oliver seems weird. "Shit," he says softly under his breath. He leans down to get his pen off the floor and sits back up. "Good morning."

"Hi."

Good morning. If Oliver is here in his capacity as my secondary jailer, then he doesn't seem like it. He hasn't made a single move to remind me that he's a threat. In the muted light of the sitting room, he looks like a slightly rough-and-tumble man. But what do I know? Nothing. I thought Decker looked innocent. I thought I was innocent.

It occurs to me that I'm really, really rumpled. I have no idea what my hair looks like and my dress is definitely not on straight. All I did was add a diamond bracelet to my look. I reach for the straps and adjust the fabric. Oliver decides he shouldn't be sitting on the sofa and stands up.

"I didn't—I hope I wasn't interrupting you," I tell him. I should have gone for the shower and fresh clothes first. There's that saying about hindsight.

"No, of course not. It's my job. Security is my job." He takes a breath and starts over. "Mr. Hades didn't want you to think you'd been left alone."

I put the back of my hand to my forehead. "Whatever would I do if I were left alone? Die, probably."

Snoop, probably. Get punished for it, probably. But not everything can be as heavy as yesterday was. I'll get crushed under the weight.

Oliver cracks a smile, which has the effect of making his scar less noticeable. "He wanted me to tell you—"

I hold up one finger and he stops, eyebrows raised. "Can you do something for me, Oliver?"

His shoulders stiffen. "That would depend on what it was."

"It's nothing wrong. Nothing Hades would be upset about, I'm sure of it." I'm not sure of anything, actually. Hades could turn good behavior into a reason for a brutal punishment, which I would then love. It's so wrong. "Can you pretend I haven't come in here yet?"

His mouth quirks. "Going back to bed?"

"Better. I bet you're going to wait here either way, right? Just—go back to what you were doing."

I go back into the bedroom to the sound of Oliver settling back on the couch and wait for the press of anxiety around my lungs. Hades wouldn't let someone untrustworthy into his private rooms. But why does he trust Oliver? I don't want to know—at least not right now. But any man who could protect Hades would have to be at least as dangerous as he is.

And yet I'm pretty sure he was doing a crossword puzzle in a newspaper.

What's more important than this latest development is my shower. Hades has put everything I might need in exactly the places I would think to look for them. Overnight, it seems, I've gotten my own drawer in his bathroom. While I'm brushing my teeth I watch myself in the mirror. Does this count as my bathroom now? Probably not. In a way, I'm on the same level as the bathroom—another piece of his sprawling property. But I get glimmers of something else when he—what did he say? When he loses control.

Freshly dressed in leggings and a tunic the color of a real poppy—this time with a pair of soft shoes, because I don't plan on spending the rest of the day in bed—I go back out to the sitting room.

Oliver folds the newspaper over and puts his pen on top. "Good morning, Persephone."

"Good morning. How's your crossword puzzle?"

It is more than surreal, having this kind of light conversation with a man who's certainly a killer at best. The only real thing in the world is Hades.

"It's good." Oliver lifts his chin. "Fine." He seems to struggle with what he's going to say next. "I'm not very good at crossword puzzles, to be frank with you."

"I'm not, either."

This drags another smile from his serious expression. "You're always in that library, reading. How could you not be good at crossword puzzles?"

It makes the hairs on the back of my neck stand up, but I'm not sure why. I've never seen Oliver in the library. I've never seen him watching at all, but he knows. Should I be terrified or comforted? If they've been watching me so closely, how could Decker have planned my escape?

Or Hades told him about you.

That's not quite as scary, but it is...unsettling. It's unsettling because I can't picture Hades having a friend. Employees, yes. Contracts, yes. but a friend? Oliver might be the only one.

"Lack of practice, I guess. My mother didn't buy a lot of puzzle books."

"Neither did mine. Got a late start." Oliver rubs his hands together. "I'm supposed to deliver a message from Mr. Hades. He left to put down some trouble in the mines, but there was something he wanted you to see."

"Okay. Where is it?" I scan the sitting room. A low sofa. Two chairs. Black chairs on a white rug. A narrow window to let in some light, but it has the same strange quality as all Hades' other windows. They must filter out the sun somehow. A tablet and a book sit on the table by the sofa. And...that's it. There's no art on the walls. No extra colors. Oliver's hair and my shirt are the brightest things in the room.

Oliver waits by the door. "Not in here, in case you hadn't already reached that conclusion."

We go out into the main hallway and make a sharp turn to the left. Surprise—another hallway. It must have been here all along, but I never noticed. At the end of the hall Oliver presses a switch in the wall. A door swings open. I suck in an enormous breath. Because on the other side of the door is the valley.

How can Hades hate the sun so much and still have such easy access to the outdoors? It's right here. All along, I thought I'd been imprisoned in miles of stone. The valley could have easily been another trick of the window. But it's real. It's here.

Oliver beckons me forward and I go, glad with every step that I put some shoes on.

There is no boundary between the door and the grass except for a short, three-inch step. I hesitate at the exit and find myself looking at Oliver for reassurance.

"It's fine." He nods into the open air. "He gave his permission."

Something in Oliver's tone makes me think that Hades gave more than permission, but I'm too dumbstruck by the sight of green to care. I take one tentative step outside the mountain. For all I wanted this, I feel...bare. Exposed. I take a half-step back. In open air like this, anyone could get to me. Decker. Zeus. Anyone.

"It's safe," says Oliver. But I'm busy taking in the steep slope of the valley, the green rise...and the small cottage at the other side. I can't believe this is here. Here, high on the mountain. The angle of the rock must be perfect for all this to have grown, or else Hades forced it to grow by brute force. Either is equally plausible, but it looks like a plain miracle to me. A breeze whips past the door, stirring my hair.

It's colder than it looks out here. Bracing. Wonderful.

A woman comes out of the cottage.

For a heart-stopping instant I'm seeing my mother. Not my mother with her hair flying behind her, but my mother as an old woman. Slightly slower. Still as confident. This person could be my mother. She's not, though—she's too old.

This is not the woman who has pinched me and locked me in my room and told me how I could die every day of my life. Who kept me inside by the force of her anger. Who kept the world from me. It's not her.

"Who is that?" I want to run back inside and slam the door and I want to run out into the valley and throw my arms around this stranger. It turns out that being out in all this green isn't simple. It's not simple at all. "Who is it, Oliver?"

"That's Eleanor." Oliver doesn't seem inclined to come out here. He looks out over the valley with me, scanning from side to side. Always checking.

A new curiosity pushes out all my tormented thoughts. "She's really old."

"Yeah."

"Did she live here before he built this place?"

Oliver lets out a short laugh. It's more of a bark than anything else. "No. That wouldn't—with all the dynamite—" He shakes his head. "No. Mr. Hades brought her with him. From home."

Home.

From *home*.

This is all...a lot. The things Hades mentions—a family, his father—they're all common concepts. They just don't seem to fit him. It wasn't too long ago that I came to the stunning realization that Hades had a childhood, he had a life—so there must have been other people in it. *Snap out of it, Persephone. You had a life, too.*

Oliver is handing me a piece of that past right now.

He blinks at me. "What?"

"I can't picture him living anywhere but here." In the next breath, I can. *We ate him alive.* All the disparate shreds of information knit together into something coherent. I can picture Hades living somewhere else. I can't picture it being good. The woman who knows more secrets goes back into her cottage, reappearing a minute later with what looks like a watering can.

"Is this—" I wave at the valley. "Is this all I get?"

"That's the other thing Hades wanted me to relay." Oliver looks mildly uncomfortable, like he knows what this means but isn't in any position to stop it. "You can go out and meet her, if you want."

18

ONCE AGAIN, I was wrong. Eleanor couldn't be my mother. But she could be my grandmother. My nerves jangle on my way across the valley.

For one thing, it's an extremely steep valley and one wrong step could send me tumbling down into the ravine at the center. That would not make a great impression. For another, she could be my grandmother. Having a grandmother is my oldest, silliest, most impossible wish. The characters in the books I read had grandmothers. Big, sprawling families. From what little I've learned from Zeus and Hades, I don't think a big family is less complicated than a little one—maybe it's worse.

But a *grandparent*. I can't imagine it.

Eleanor sees me coming and waves.

"Hi," I shout across the breeze. When the wind dies down it's plenty warm and summery, but the moment it picks up again it reminds me that we are almost on the top of a mountain. It's frigid up here under the best of circumstances.

As I approach, Eleanor bends to pluck one flower from the grass, then another. What am I going to say? What am I going to do? What kind of conversations do people have with grandparents? I don't know. I've never had one. My mother's creepy old assistant is the oldest person I've ever known, and he got replaced by Decker, who then...

Best not to think about that now.

Best to just breathe in the clean, fresh air and feel the sun on my face.

Up here, it's like the summer is set back in time, to several weeks into spring. No humidity hangs in the air. The world on the mountain is just waking up. Under my feet, the earth still has hard chunks beneath the grass. My feet would freeze without my shoes. That's okay. I don't need to be barefoot to appreciate this. This is not a fantasy—this is real, it's real, thank god it's real.

I come level with Eleanor and fold my hands into my sleeves. The blue sky is an upside-down bowl above us, the jagged edges of the mountain keeping us in. That's for the best. If I could see down the side I'd get vertigo and fall.

"Good morning, Persephone." Eleanor straightens up and smiles at me, and her smile is warmer than the sun. She has a cute, crinkled face. She's so old, but so...sturdy? Yes. That's the right word.

"Oh, I'm sorry." She waves a hand in front of her face. "I'm being entirely rude. I should have pretended not to know your name until we were properly introduced."

I laugh out loud, the breeze carrying the sound off into the valley. "It would be weirder if you did that, I promise." So much excitement has filtered into my blood that I don't care. It makes me brave. "Everyone here knows who I am."

"I doubt that." She bends to pick another flower and comes up again with another smile. "Luther tends to play his cards close to his chest. Then again, rumors do spread quickly in a place like this."

"I'd like to hear more of them." I sound so foolish,

but there's nothing to do but press on. "I would really like to talk to you."

"Then talk to me." Eleanor heads back toward the cottage and I fall into step beside her. "We can talk as long as you have time, but I have work to do."

I'm fully ready for her to head around the back of the cottage—work with flowers happens outside, unless she has a greenhouse—but Eleanor opens the front door and steps inside without looking back at me. This is—this is something else. I have no sense of being a guest, or an outsider.

"Keep up," she calls from somewhere toward the back of the cottage. It reminds me a lot of my mother's cottage. Same whitewashed walls, same braided rug. Simple wood furniture. A bright kitchen with a faded dishrag hung on the stove. My heart aches for it. I close the door on another gust of wind and head through the kitchen and living room, following the sound of her voice.

I find Eleanor in a back room. A huge back room. It's a smaller version of the rotunda by Hades' train station, with the same dark marble. When I get far enough in a hidden door glides closed behind us. Eleanor flicks on a light, but the light comes from the wrong direction. The floor. It's a luminescent glow under our feet.

What the hell is she up to?

"Your house looks a lot smaller from the outside."

She wrinkles her nose. "Doesn't it? Luther insisted on a direct connection. I wouldn't call that warren of hallways direct, but you can see where his space begins and mine gets bigger." Eleanor laughs at her own joke. Oh, I like her. It's an instant, comfortable affection. It's probably not allowed, to like someone so quickly, but too late—it's already happened.

Eleanor looks down into a planter in front of her, the top edge at waist height. Seeing the first one makes the rest of them come into focus. There are forty of them, maybe fifty, set into slots along the outside of the circular room. And what's in the planters makes perfect sense, except for the weird lights and the dark.

Plants.

Flowers.

"I'm growing flowers." She laughs softly to herself. "As you can see."

I can, but what I can't see is why. It doesn't seem half as risky to ask questions here as it does in the light of Hades' bedroom. Hades wouldn't have sent me out here if he didn't want me to ask questions. Or maybe he would have. Either way, I have to know about these flowers—flowers that bloom in the dark.

"What are they for?"

Eleanor moves to the next planter. Waters. Does something to the soil. Pats it down.

"He likes flowers."

He. Likes. Flowers.

Why is it that everything people say in this place seem like little bombs, meant to explode what I thought I knew? My mind does a hasty struggle between what I know—that Hades does not care about flowers—and what Eleanor knows, because she's known him a lot longer than I have. Jealousy burns the back of my throat.

No—no. I refuse it. I'm not going to be jealous of an old lady, even if she does know some fact about Hades that I would never have guessed. One glass poppy does not indicate that a person likes flowers. Now I'm questioning everything.

"The thing about flowers here..." The watering can flashes in the light at the next planter down. "They have to be resilient enough for the lights. If you ask me, it's more a problem of timing than anything else. Everything must be exactly right..." She snaps her fingers to indicate *exactly right*. "Otherwise, they can't stand up to the environment. "Between you and me, I'm not often successful."

"But you keep trying? Is it...is it a contract with him?"

"No, no." Eleanor's fingers move down into the dirt. A sprouted plant comes up, and she moves it a few inches to the right. "He gave me something to do. He thinks I'll be lonely without a project."

Who is the man she's talking about? Not the Hades I know.

But then I think of the pomegranate. Of the fury in his face when he discovered I wasn't eating. The library. The books...

"Are you? Lonely, I mean."

"How could I be lonely? I'm getting constant visitors. Luther visits me—oh, once or twice a week. And the others are in and out for the things they need."

"The others?"

"Don't you live in this mountain too, my dear?" Eleanor winks at me, and I have no idea what that wink is supposed to mean. Hopefully the dim light hides the heat in my cheeks.

"I've been preoccupied."

Pressure accumulates at my breastbone. She's going to tell me something else that rocks the world off its axis, isn't she? I brace myself.

"Ah."

The urge to explain rears up. Whenever my mother was angry I had to choke out this same, stupid urge. Explanations never made her less furious. Explanations didn't convince her to take the lock off my door or send me back to school.

"The others." Her gaze goes to the shadowy dark at the end of the room, where those hallways connecting her to Hades' fortress must be. "Most of the ones in his mines are like him, in one way or another."

My head shakes in spite of myself. "That's impossible. Nobody's like him." Nobody is as cruel or as demanding or as passionate. Nobody.

"The light hurts them, too."

I grab on to a nearby planter and use it to steady myself. What fresh vertigo hell is this. "Eleanor, are you joking? All those people...they can't be like him. Someone would have done something by now." There would be...a drug. A treatment. A cure.

Maybe there is a drug.

Maybe Hades left something out on his map.

"I'll admit that very few have such an...intense physical reaction to the sunlight." Eleanor clicks her tongue and moves three planters down. "Very few. Many more find it intolerable for other reasons. Not the sun, but—you know what I mean. The world. They sign their contracts with him and then they don't have to go back."

I've heard those rumors before—that people go to the mountain and never come out again. They went willingly. I don't know how much more of this conversation I can handle right now, honestly. I'm ready to sit down hard on the grass outside and let the breeze strip away the confused heat in my cheeks and the horrible divide in my brain. The fact that I need Hades doesn't make him a good man. He's a dangerous man, the cruelest person I've ever met.

Eleanor's not done, and she's not lying, either. She's just talking. It's a casual truth. The way I imagine a grandmother would talk to a granddaughter.

"Now, with Luther...It wasn't so bad when he was younger. Most times, I could keep him out of his father's way."

When he was younger. He'd have to have been very young for a woman like Eleanor to be able to meaningfully control him in any way, and my mind runs into another end. Of course he was a little boy once. I just can't picture it. I don't want to follow the breadcrumbs that lead from those years to this one. To a man like Hades.

"You've known him since he was a child?"

"Of course, dear heart. I was his nanny."

My heart sinks, stomach going cold. I don't want to understand what she's telling me. We ate him alive. This is like unraveling a blanket. The intricate stitches reveal many more layers to the fabric than can be seen from the surface. A woman who cared for him, doing her best to keep him away from his own father...the rage that must have been involved...

"What would—what would his father have to do with the sun?"

"It's better if an angry man can't use it for punishment. Now it's only Demeter's flowers standing between him and—"

A voice calls out from the murky black. Eleanor puts down the watering can and pulls me into a brief hug. She smells like the mountain breeze and a gentle powder, and I have to hold myself back from putting my head down on her shoulder to cry. Her papery palms come up to meet my cheeks. "Come back another day, Persephone. I'll teach you to make flowers grow for him."

19

PERSEPHONE

Hᴀᴅᴇs ɪsɴ'ᴛ in his room when I come back in, so I keep the wind in my hair and try to imagine that the sun is still on my face. A small window in the library helps, plus the discovery of the book he's left me. At first glance it's nothing out of the ordinary, but when I pick it up the cover crackles.

It's covered in plastic.

This isn't something he already owned, it's something from a library.

A stamp on the inside names its owner: The New York Public Library.

I laugh out loud. "What?"

There's no answer, nobody here, but...how? How did he steal books from that faraway library for me?

Settling in with this book—an adventure story about spaceships and a coordinated alien attack—gives my thoughts a little order. They're still in a kind of disarray, one here, another over there—but at least all of them are gathered in the same place.

It takes me a few paragraphs to become aware of Hades standing in the door with a strange, almost soft expression on his face. As soon as I do I wonder how I ever missed him—he takes up most of the doorframe and the way he watches me is hot enough to burn. Should I stand up? No, I don't think so. I shove the book onto the table by my armchair.

"I met Eleanor today. Oliver said that it was okay."

He comes into the room, all long lines and expensive, dark clothes. Hades' face hardens. "Good. Then you can get some fresh air without being unaccompanied."

Something happened to him today. Maybe I wasn't observant enough to notice it before, but I notice it now. The thin ring of blue in his eyes is my first hint. The second is the rough set of his jaw. Like he's been grinding his teeth. A memory of the crisp breeze dances over my cheeks.

"We had a nice conversation." I sit up straight and tall in the armchair, like he's a headmaster out of one of my books. The quiet pulse between my legs started before he walked in the room but it intensifies now, the closer he gets. He clouds my mind. Makes it too hard to stop talking. "Oliver didn't tell me that she was your nanny."

Another flash in his eyes, an emotion gone too fast to do anything more than send a shiver down my spine. "She was."

Stop, stop. Stop talking, don't say anything...

I can't stop. There's a dark, dirty part of me that wants to goad him into punishing me. But most of me wants to press against the boundaries he's built up around himself. If what Eleanor says isn't true, he'll brush it off with a cruel word. If it is, then I'll have learned something. I want to please him and I want to push him in equal measure. I want to be a good girl and a twisted little slut.

"She told me about your father."

His face turns to stone, gaze sharper than all of his diamonds.

"I shouldn't have said anything." I try to swim up from the intoxicating haze of looking at him. "It was a mista—"

His hand comes down across the front of my throat and cuts off the word and my breath. It's a glancing blow, long enough to get my attention. He has it. He has all of my attention. With the other hand he pins my wrists above my head on the chair, stopping only to run his fingers over my new bracelet. Is he regretting it?

"No, Persephone. Go on. Tell me about my father."

While he says this he tears my leggings off, ripping them in the process. My panties come next. My socks. The bralette I found in a drawer in the closet. He leaves the tunic, which only makes it worse when he shoves it up around my neck.

I can't tell him about his father because I'm struggling to catch my breath. Hades steals all the air from any room he enters, and the only way to get it back is to beg him for it. My body is begging him for it. I'm a house fire, burning up underneath him.

The last thing I need is more oxygen. It's the only thing I want.

He knocks my knees apart with his free hand, letting them fall over the arms of the chair, and then he twists his fingers into me.

"Do you need to be reminded of my belt, Persephone?"

He's so cold, uncaring. Harsh. Nothing makes me hotter than when he's like this. He curls his fingers and I clench down on them with a gasp. Hades does it again and one of my knees slips from the arm of the chair. He puts it back in place with a mean slap.

"She—she—she said that he would punish you with the sun." The things he's doing with his fingers— god, I can't, I can't. Hades winds me up with a detached, exacting precision. His only goal is to make me come, and right now. "She said—"

The first orgasm hits me in mid-sentence and I lose the rest of it.

Every time I think that nothing can ever be more humiliating, nothing can ever turn me on more, Hades finds a way.

Nothing can be worse than this. It's not dark,

there's no cover, and his fingers are still inside. Working. Twisting. Curling. What's he doing? Am I supposed to be asking a question? I decide to ask one.

"I don't understand what she meant. I don't know what she meant."

"Do you ever stare at the sun?"

The inside of me is so sensitive that another one is already starting again. I'm pinned in place by his hands and by the chair and there's nowhere for my hips to go.

"No. It's dangerous. You're not supposed to look —look—"

He strokes harder, and I swear I can feel the tip of his fingernail touching a part of me that feels like a live wire. Like a spark, a cascade of sparks, a wild-fire. Hades watches me while I come again, short and hard.

"You're not supposed to look at the sun," I finish.

"And if you were stupid, you might try it." Those fingers. Again. Again. I can't even begin to get away. My legs are too heavy to lift from the arms of the chair. "If you stared long enough, it would feel like a knife in your eye sockets. It would feel like an icepick through your temple. It would feel like jagged rocks boring into your skull."

He makes me come a third time, and this time, when it's almost over, he adds a thumb to my clit and rubs in slow, easy circles until I scream.

"See how it works? How quickly pleasure turns to pain?"

"I do, I see it."

The rest of what I'm trying to say turns into nonsense. Whimpers. Cries. His thumb is relentless. I had no idea a light touch could feel so good, or hurt so much. His fingers twist again and I can't resist him. I couldn't stop myself from coming even if I tried. It tears through me like the edge of a knife. I can't catch my breath. Beads of sweat gather on my collarbone.

"If you start with pain…" Hades curls his fingers, deliberate, slow, torturous. It's like him in every way. In the most extreme ways. "If you start with pain it turns into more pain until finally all pleasure is consumed. Until every sensation could eat you alive. Look at me. Look at me."

This orgasm—this will be the one to consume me. I'm barely alive at the end of it, hanging on by a thread. The blue in his eyes is almost gone. "This is what light does to me, in all its forms. I can delay it with special lights, but it always ends like this. There is no cure. There is no fix."

My heart breaks for him while my body breaks apart under his hands. The beginning of a scream bursts out of me but I bite it back. If I start screaming again now, I might not stop—and I'm getting what I wanted. I wanted to know more about him. I know it now down to the marrow.

"And...it...hurts...you?"

"Every waking moment, unless I get what I need."

He offers me one moment of reprieve in the form of tracing his thumb around the outside of my pussy. It's not enough to breathe, not with his fingers in as deep as they'll go. He's going to do it again, he's going to do it again—

His fingers curl.

This isn't so much an orgasm as a wretched, screaming peak. Words fly apart into senseless sounds and the universe narrows to his hand. Curling. Stroking. I have to fight my way out of it, out of darkening vision and not enough air. When I do, Hades looks completely calm, as if he's not forcing me to orgasm as payment, as punishment.

I take the biggest breath of my life. "What is it that you need?"

He cocks his head to the side, looking down at me. We could be anywhere. A meeting room in the city. A headmaster's office at a college. He's worked years for this, hasn't he? He spent years learning to hide an excruciating pain. He had to. He didn't have any other choice. The fragments of my heart snap again. It's not Hades I feel sorry for. It's that little boy. And a little girl I knew once, who could never get out of her mother's fields.

"Are you sure you want to buy that information?"

"Yes," I hiss. I'm shaking, an earthquake made human.

"Very well."

I don't realize he pulled back until his hand slams back into me, his fingers ready to destroy me. Hades gives no mercy. He drives me into another electric burn of an orgasm. I feel it up to my fingertips. I'm not trying to pull away, not trying to wrench my wrists away from him—it's my base instincts. If I am the universe then this is also the end of the universe. It's the end of me. It rushes up in a tall wave, inescapable, and I take one final breath before I go under.

It's a long while before I resurface. How long, I don't know. My hearing comes back first. Wind plays on the narrow window, testing the glass. Hades breathes nearby. Vision is next.

He's watching me.

When I blink up at him he eases his fingers out of me. Even that small movement is too much and I arch back on the chair, jaw locked tight, making small noises that I won't let into the air.

He takes a deep breath, lets it out.

"There are certain plants only Demeter knows how to grow. The pills she makes can keep the worst of the pain at bay for a few hours at a time."

Hades releases my wrist. I'm wrecked, spent. I'm going to need his help to get out of the chair. If I give it everything I've got I might be able to walk to the bedroom, but I'm betting I'll end up in a heap on the floor.

He keeps his eyes on me, in this horrible, exposed position, while he undoes the buttons at his wrists. Undoes his belt. He can't be doing that. It's a dim thought and it falls apart in the face of all the evidence. Hades is shoving his shirtsleeves up to his elbows. He is stepping out of his pants. He's letting the huge iron length of him out into the air.

He is stroking a hand over one of my knees, then the other, and then he's bending down to put his big hands just above my knees on the arms of the chair. It takes his weight. It's made to.

"There's only one other thing that has that effect," Hades comments. His lips are an inch from mine. He brushes them against me. He hasn't kissed me up until now, but my lips still feel bruised and swollen. All of me is so sensitive I could die.

"What is it?" I don't have enough energy to work up true fear.

Hades thrusts himself inside me and leans down to brush a stinging kiss to my cheek, whispering one word in my ear: "You."

20

Oliver paces back and forth in my main living room, staring at the windows like we're in danger of imminent attack. I'm quickly running out of patience for his performance, even if it is probably justified. A summer storm lashes at the window. Lighting bolts strike out over the countryside. Oliver paces. Three, four, five, six steps. Turn. Another set of steps.

"No one is going to scale the mountain and burst through the window, Oliver. Not in the next fifteen minutes anyway. Sit down."

"I can't." He crosses his arms over his chest and I get a glimpse of the man he used to be—the man I forced onto the train by his shirt collar when he tried to get back to the city the first time. "Something's coming. It's not right out there."

What's not right is me, standing here with Oliver, instead of shutting the door on the world with Persephone. I'm not accustomed to hiding from problems.

This one, however, is unsolvable.

"Did you try getting through to Zeus's people today?"

"Yes." Oliver runs the pad of his thumb over his other four fingernails, back and forth. "Even the people outside his circle aren't answering. It's like the city's gone dead. Or dark. If you would just let me—"

"No." For the last day, while I've been settling unrest in the mines—no doubt because that stupid fuck tried to whip everyone into a rebellion—Oliver has been popping up to ask if he can go to the city and scout things out. He cannot. "You're needed here."

"We need more information."

"What matters is that I crossed a line with Zeus." Damn it, he's rubbing off on me. I find myself in front of the same window Oliver had been looking out of. "Because he crossed the fucking line with me. It's always been a tacit agreement of ours that we don't settle scores using law enforcement. There's no telling what he might do."

"Buy his way out," Oliver guesses. "Why wouldn't he?"

"There's a prosecutor in the city who could complicate that for him." The name of the prosecutor was the last news to reach me out of the city. Oliver's correct—it seems like the whole place has been leveled. And since I'm not the one who did that, it must have been Zeus.

I watch the rain on the glass until Conor gets up from his bed and comes to my side. His tail flaps onto the floor in a quick heartbeat rhythm. The sound, light as it is, drills into my brain. I'm trying to ration the pills for the inevitable disaster. Rationing doesn't work out nearly as well when I have to light up the diamond mines. The people down there take the dark as an excuse to go wild with the least provocation. How quickly they forget what I've given them.

"It's rain, Conor. It's nothing. Go back to bed."

Conor inches closer to my leg. It has no urgency to it. The dog wants to be close, not get me out of the room, though if this conversation goes on much longer he'll start to insist. This need for closeness isn't altogether unexpected. No one, including me, has been able to convince him to rest and relax. He was shot, and he will not recuperate nicely in his bed except for during the night. It must mean he's healing.

"What should we do?" Oliver's reflection moves back and forth in a smaller area. "How the hell do we prepare? They're not going to wait forever."

"What's your read on the situation, then?" This is part of his tenure here. He's not going to be empty muscle—I have enough of that at my disposal. If Oliver is going to pace around in my private quarters when I'd rather be fucking Persephone then he needs to have something to bring to the table.

"That Zeus and Demeter are planning something."

I think of that circle I drew around the marks of our properties. My mountain has always been the anchor, the linchpin. Is it still true if Zeus has sat for a comparatively small amount of time in a federal prison? He has enough friends that he should be able to weasel himself out eventually. On the other hand—the prosecutor.

"Zeus and Demeter make lots of plans. Almost none of them concern me."

Oliver throws a look at me. He must not know I can see him. "You crossed a line. You said it yourself. Even if you were justified, it happened."

"And I can't un-cross it. I can't un-send federal agents into his illegal whorehouse. It's not my fault our father trafficked in businesses on the wrong side of the law." I stroke Conor's head. "We're beyond that now. I wouldn't undo it if I could, not when it meant getting Persephone back. If you don't have a plausible suggestion, then leave me in peace."

"You should shut down the train."

That, and only that, makes me turn away from the window to see if he's kidding. It's impossible to know for sure with all the rain.

Oliver's serious.

He stands in the center of the room with his chin slightly raised, hands in his pockets. When I first met him, the act of looking at him would send him into a defensive crouch. He was so ready for life to lay him out flat that he started seeking out situations where that would be the only possible result. He's come a long way, the crazy bastard.

"Do you know what you're asking?"

"You'll buy yourself some time."

"That's not how it will play out."

Shutting down the train is easy in theory and disastrous in practice. The train is what supplies the mountain with all the things necessary to feed and clothe the people who work here permanently. Of all of them, I'm the most insulated—I have stores of everything I need.

Almost everything. But whether I shut down the train or not, the fact that I've taken Persephone is going to be a bigger problem in sixteen days, give or take. It's a fact I've been conveniently ignoring. It's easier to ignore when there are willing distractions waiting in my bedroom.

"There are private cars, Oliver. They could fly if they wanted to." This hypothetical includes Zeus and Demeter and whoever else they choose to bring with them—if that's really what happens. The two of them coming alone would be a waste of time and energy. I'd sooner barricade the mountain than let them step foot here.

"But they're not going to fly," Oliver insists. "They're gathering an army."

"An army." I look at him long enough that most people would look away, but he doesn't. "You think my foolish fuck of a brother has managed to hire an army from federal prison?"

"Is he in federal prison?"

"I assume so. But even if he's not, he'll have limited access while he's under investigation." Someone will have to investigate him, probably that prosecutor. It will take some time. Oliver's fear isn't justified for the moment.

"I think you should stop the trains. That's what I think." He rubs a hand over the back of his head. Conor pushes at my leg. It's time to go. "Obviously I'll defend this place no matter what you decide."

"Good. Wake me if there's another problem in the mines."

"I will." He's lying—he won't. We both know that he'll settle things himself or lock the troublemakers in until I'm available in the morning. Oliver only disturbs me at night when there's a real need. He goes out through the door and locks it behind him. I had that system installed the last time Demeter's crops went bad and I pressed my luck with some floodlights down in the mines.

"Bed, Conor." He darts ahead of me, anxious to get to the bedroom. My skin feels raw tonight. If Oliver is right, then acting sooner will help us. Causing unrest in the diamond mines, however, will not help anyone—and if that unrest spills over to the rest of the mountain, Persephone could be at risk. I can't fucking stand the thought.

A shadow comes out from my office.

A shadow shaped curiously like Persephone.

My hand goes to my belt. "What the fuck were you doing in there?"

Conor stops at the end of the hall and circles back to her.

"I wasn't doing anything." She twists at the hem of her nightgown, a gauzy white thing that I had put in the closet because it will rip apart without hurting her. "I learned my lesson on that one."

"I'm not blind, Persephone. I can see you coming out of that room. You are forbidden to go in there."

"I think technically you just said not to go through your desk," she tries, eyes darting from one end of the hall to the other. Where does she think she's going to go? "But I wasn't doing that. I swear, I wasn't. I—I wasn't doing anything wrong." Persephone plants her feet, eyes flashing, and it breaks me. She won't fucking forget this. She will not.

I make it two full steps before Conor leaps in front of her, baring his teeth. Growling. Conor snaps at me, his ears back.

After growing up with my father I assured myself there were no surprises left. I'm not used to the intensity of shock. My own fucking dog, growling at me. He's ready to bite me. For her.

I step back. "Damn it, Conor."

Conor watches me, sharp teeth a warning in the light coming off Persephone's nightgown.

I put my hands down by my sides, palms out. "Fine." My own dog. Is there no one left who won't betray me? Christ. "I told you to protect her. Good boy."

A snap of my fingers brings him back to me, a hitch in his step. This dog. He thinks he can get away with murder. He obviously doesn't know that I'm the only one capable of that kind of killing. I spend perhaps longer than necessary petting Conor's head and scratching between his ears. I can't have a dog that won't protect her at any cost. Conor's already proven that. But I'll be damned if my own fucking dog thinks I'm a threat.

I am, of course, a threat. He's right about that. But not in that way. Not for Persephone.

When I look up from the dog I find Persephone still standing in the middle of the hallway, watching me intently. Her hair looks windblown. It's a beautiful mess. The sight of it scrabbles at my ribs and squeezes my heart in its fist. The siren song of telling secrets gestures to me from open water, looking at her. And in the same moment, I know I never can. Persephone spends all her time trying to find the truth. I can't fuck or punish that desire out of her, sadly for her. The truth is a razor. It can slice open your skin and bleed you out before you have time to be afraid. In my experience, the truth means a slow, hollow death.

And she is not a creature of death. She belongs in

green fields. In sunshine. The hem of her dress lifts as if caught by an unseen breeze. A vision of a clear blue sky appears in my memory, and when I look at her it doesn't hurt at all.

I shake myself out of it. Fuck—my grasp on this day is slipping.

"Explain yourself." She bites her lip. "Before I change my mind."

"I was bringing you flowers," she says.

21

PERSEPHONE

IT RAINS for almost a week before the sun comes back out. I can sense it behind the windows, and when I wake up without Hades I know it's time to go see Eleanor. Rainy day visits are possible, but...wet. And cold. The one time I tried it he made me go without clothes for the rest of the day to appreciate the warmth. And other things. There are always other things. Oliver, tastefully, stayed away on that day.

I roll over and stretch in the bed, my hand knocking against something *else* on his pillow. A jewelry box with an intricate diamond pattern.

I pull the small chest onto my lap. The diamonds form the shape of the sun.

The sun—that's for me. The rest of the box—a matte surface, deep black—is for him. It matches his bedroom. It's something for me to keep in his bedroom.

I don't need a jewelry box for one bracelet and the few other pieces he's given me. This is a plan. For a *future*.

My breath catches at the thought of it. I choose a spot in the closet for the box and keep the bracelet on. But before I leave, I make a detour into the guest bedroom. The necklaces he gave me are where I left them a century ago, on a small shelf next to the bed. The new box is the perfect home for them. I'm pretty sure this is what swooning feels like, but I can't stand in his closet for the rest of the day. I need to go out.

A run across the field makes my heart beat fast and strong. I can only hope that Hades isn't watching. He'd be pissed if I broke an ankle. God knows what he'd do if that happened. I'm curious. I can't say I'm not. But a broken bone seems like too high a price, even for me. Still, I jog up to the door of Eleanor's house and knock.

No answer.

She must be in the back, tending her plants. I open the door and kick my shoes off at the mat. It feels strangely very good to kick my shoes off on a cheery doormat. That's not my life now, but this part of it still is. The mat is, and the new sandals are. They're ugly leather things and Hades had them sent here so I don't track dirt through Eleanor's house. I slip into them and go back to her growing room.

Eleanor's looking closely into one of the planter's at the back. "It finally stopped raining," she says. "I'm glad. I missed you."

I put my hand over my heart and bask in the simple kindness of her missing me. There are no strings attached when Eleanor misses me. Can you imagine? "I missed you, too. How are the flowers?"

"You're a miracle girl," she says, only a little ruefully. "I can't believe you got those other ones to bloom. What did Luther think?"

Hades thought they were worth a dangerously hard fuck that make me sleep through half the morning. I managed not to tell him that I looked in one single drawer in his desk. The papers were gone. None of this is appropriate conversation for Eleanor. "He liked them."

"Good. Good. I'm hopeful about these ones, here. They might last longer inside the house." She claps her hands together. "I need to gather some plants today. Are you interested in a walk?"

We go back out in the sun, baskets in our hand, and I'm living in a complete fantasy. Eleanor, the white clouds, the green grass...and the flowers. Remember this, I think as I pick them next to her. She asks me idle questions on our way down to the ravine and across to the other side of the valley. I get so caught up in the feel of the grass—cold stalks, warm earth —that I miss the first part of her question. It has to do with plans.

"My only plan has been to visit the New York Public Library. But now I'm not sure how that would work out."

"It's a public library, dear one. You simply travel there and walk in during regular business hours, like all libraries."

Eleanor pauses, going through her basket and rear- ranging the flowers.

"Right, but..." But my vision of the New York Public Library isn't the same as it used to be. Now it includes standing there with Hades, which means standing there with Conor. I can't think of a single scenario where Hades would let me walk into an enormous building in New York City by myself. "If we went..." It's a good thing there's plenty to look at out here. *We* makes my face hotter than a sunburn. "If we went, then Hades would want to take Conor. He always has his dog with him. Almost always, unless Conor stays with me."

Eleanor raises her eyebrows. "He leaves his dog with you? Alone?"

"Yes," I say brightly, but I feel like the ground is unsteady now, the angle of the ravine too steep. I don't normally talk about Hades—not with anyone except Oliver, and then only to find out where he's gone while I'm asleep. It's too tempting not to talk about this. "He seems very...attached...to Conor." Eleanor nods slowly through this, which gives me the courage to go on. "It's almost like he helps him. With his eyes."

She laughs. "Your face is so red. It's not a secret, Persephone."

"He never talks about it."

"Of course not." Eleanor is so casual about this that I fall silent for a while and concentrate on picking flowers. Of course not? That doesn't sound good. "That doesn't change the fact that the dog has a sixth sense. He can warn Luther when he's going to have an attack."

I try to pretend I've been distracted, half-listening, but my heartbeat is so loud in my ears that I doubt I'm pulling it off. "An attack?"

Because...no. A man like Hades is not susceptible to weakness. He hates weakness. He'd rather die than admit there was any soft part of him. This cannot be true.

Eleanor looks at me meaningfully. "I'm sure you've seen it."

"No, I—I guess not."

She clicks her tongue. "Sooner or later."

That leaves a gnawing pit in my stomach. What does she mean, an attack? What would that look like? What would happen? He took an unbelievable risk coming into the city to get me, I realize between heartbeats. And if my mother's the one who makes the pills he needs, then...then he's really screwed. There's no other way to put it. She likes her revenge. My mother has dishtowels with poppies on them but she should have a hand-lettered sign that says an eye for an eye.

I choose flowers at random, no longer really seeing them. My lungs feel half-functioning. My lips go next. We need to change the topic to anything else, and fast.

Nothing comes to mind. Hades is my new center of gravity, and even when he's not here, he pulls me toward him.

"He seems worried about Conor, in a way." Dogs. We can talk about dogs. Pets are a safe topic, as long as we avoid the fact that Conor was very recently shot. "Hades is always watching him. It's safe in the mountain, though. Nothing else is going to happen to Conor."

"Yes, well, that's an old fear of his. Justified, too. What do you think of this bloom?" Eleanor holds up a blue flower.

"The petals look a little off to me." She agrees and throws it back into the ravine. "He's afraid of his pets dying? All pets die, though, surely...surely he'd be prepared for that." I search my memory for a time when I believed that pets would be invincible. If I did, I can't remember it. "We had dogs at my mother's house. Cats, too. They all die eventually."

I flinch, hiding it by bending to pick a perfect purple flower near my toes. They all die eventually. It's not so strange for people to love their pets. It's only strange for Hades. And here I am, digging into his past with fingernails out. The more I get of him, the more I want.

"I'm sure they did." Eleanor stops and looks up at the clouds. "But your mother didn't kill them herself, did she?"

I couldn't be more mortified and more heartbroken than if she'd stripped off all my clothes right here and left me to run home in the stiff breeze. Eleanor would never do that—she never would. But I've finally done it. I went too far. I'm the idiot who goes stomping around in a battlefield and acts surprised when her foot gets blown off.

"No, she didn't. Who—" I can't get to the end of the question without dissolving into tears.

"His father did. Whenever they'd fight." Eleanor reaches up and toys with the collar of her thick cotton shirt. Her eyes have gone far away, the blue of the sky reflected there. "He was always so hopeful that one would work out. That he could hide them long enough, or——" She swallows and waves it down. "It never did work out, of course. Not until that man finally died."

Died——or was killed? I don't want to know. Whatever Hades did to him, whatever happened to him, he deserved it.

On the way back to Eleanor's house I try, mostly unsuccessfully, to get rid of the deep ache in my chest, in my belly. It hurts to understand him. God, it hurts. He must feel so wretched and broken. He must think he has to hide everything good about himself. Or maybe it's too late for him to tell the difference. This is no sunny field on a summer day. This is a lifetime of anguish.

And I traded myself for it. This is what I bought.

"Don't try to stop me, Oliver. I'm going."

Oliver does his job well, and I can see how much it pains him to even consider going against Hades' orders. "I'll call him," he says. "I'll call him and I'll tell him to come back."

I draw myself up to my full height, which is still quite a bit less than Oliver's. "Get out of my way."

Something shifts in his expression. For the first time, with Eleanor's words ringing in my ears and the sunspots still in my eyes, I don't feel like a prisoner, or an asset. I feel like a queen. This is what queens do. They're equals to their husbands or wives, and they don't let the staff stop them from doing what they need to do.

And what I need to do is talk to Hades. He has to know what I know.

Oliver steps aside.

I go out the doors into the main part of Hades' mountain fortress.

This is going to cause a stir.

The halls are filled with people huddled in the alcoves and whispering to each other. Let them look. Let them see me breaking his rules, if that's what I have to do to prove that I can handle him. When he knows I can bear him—when he really knows it—then he'll be able to let me all the way in. We won't be joined by paperwork between us and life-and-death deals. It'll be something real and timeless. I'll never think of the stupid New York Public Library again, as long as I can make him see.

People move out of my way on the long walk across the fortress. I should've worn different shoes but it's too late for that kind of regret. I should have done a lot of things, like changed my clothes, or put on makeup, or brushed out my hair. But here I am.

Nobody stops me at the giant doors to Hades' office. At the last minute I pick up the pace so I'm almost at a run when I go inside, heart beating out of my chest, pulse singing with blue skies and facts I never should have known. I ignore, with all my might, the lump in my throat and the wreckage of my soul. He'll put it back together somehow. We'll both do it.

"I'm sorry." I'm too loud, too sudden. Hades stands silhouetted in front of the windows that give him a panoramic view of the factory floor, his head bowed over a tablet. The blue light catches his face as he raises his head. Oh, shit. He's not in a good mood. His shoulders are all tension, his hands tight on the sides of the tablet. One look communicates exactly how much I've disobeyed him. It's an apocalyptic amount. My tongue sticks to the roof of my mouth. "I'm sorry," I say again, but even my lowered voice is overwhelming for the space. The sound of the wind outside, rushing around the mountain, hasn't fully left my ears. "For everything that happened to you. For everything that...still happens to you."

Concentration drops away from his face. It's hard to see him, with all the light behind us, but I get terrifying flashes. His jaw tightens. There's no color left in his eyes. His anger is a heat wave, an oncoming storm. I've run from storms before, but I'm not going to run from this one.

His grip tightens on the tablet and then he hurls it toward the window. *Don't run, don't run.* It bounces off the window and the screen shatters on the floor. Hades doesn't look at it, and neither do it—because I'm transfixed by what's happening on his face. I've never seen him run through so many emotions, so fast I can't identify them. But they feel like fear. And pain. And...relief? But all of them are crushed under the force of his anger.

Hades strips off his jacket while he crosses the floor toward me. I rock up on the balls of my feet and come back down. Don't run. Keep breathing. The jacket falls. One of his buttons comes off when he shoves his sleeves up. Then he's breaking over me, an icy cold front. My feet come off the floor and from this close, there's no denying his fury.

He's wordless with it. Another first that's terrifying in its uniqueness. He always has something to say. Not this time.

I'm bent over the desk before I have time to catch my breath or my balance, the glass surface coming up to meet me and crushing the air from my lungs. Hades takes one breath. It steadies him enough to speak while he pulls one arm behind my back, then another. A familiar tension around my wrists—his tie. He's tying me up. I struggle out of instinct and his palm pushes me back down.

"We had a deal, Persephone." Oh, god, he's going to snap. "You're skirting the terms of our deal."

My pants come off, and panties. A drawer opens. A drawer? All of me goes tense and hot. I'm already bound. I already want this. But it doesn't stop the chill of not know what's going to happen.

"Punish me, then," I tell him breathlessly.

"What the fuck do you think I'm doing?"

He spreads me apart next, perfunctory, humiliating. Wide. And then something cold and slick makes contact. A vicious, visceral flashback to the train rears up and slaps me. I know exactly what he's going to do. He can't do it. He can't, he can't. It'll never work.

"I think you're teaching me a lesson." Anything to delay, even shaky words that don't quite make sense. Words that he never asked for.

"I'm collecting payment. You're overdue, you little thief. You're a fucking brat, and you know it."

His finger comes next. I have no way to stop him and it's terrifying and wonderful—it's what I wanted. But the pendulum swings toward terrifying and I squeeze tight, trying to keep him out. Not there, not there. No, no—

Another finger. There's just not enough room. My lungs flatten, refuse to take in a breath. It's so wrong, what he's doing. This is worse than when he made me come over and over, this is worse. Two fingers in a tight space and I can't get used to him. I rock uselessly against the desk in the half-inch of leeway he's given me. I'm getting nowhere. He won't stop.

"You can steal from me. You can dig into my past for secrets. But I meant what I said, Persephone. You. Will. Pay."

He takes his fingers out and pushes them back in. How long have I been crying? Another tear splashes against the glass below me. It's too much. Too much. More lube, cold and slippery. More fingers. His other hand pins my wrists to my back. It's so sexy I can't catch my breath and so embarrassing, so awful. Wrong. Wrong. Wrong. Wrong is a drumbeat that makes my face red and the tears come faster. It makes wetness gather between my legs, where he won't touch.

Another panicked tear splashes onto the desk and the next moment the fingers are gone. Something much bigger is pushing against me. It's him, it's him, and he will never, ever fit. Hades lets go of my wrists and strokes his hands down the outside of my hips. Is he going to force it? The answer is almost certainly yes.

"Open up for me.". The command filters down through an ugly, wheezing sob, but I hope he doesn't stop. I am a sick and twisted slut and I don't want him to stop. He follows with a sharp slap to my ass.

"I don't know how," I plead. "Please, don't."

He strokes across my back—*easy, easy*—and then that hand moves around to the front of me and delves between my legs. I cannot fathom how I got to this place in my life that this situation—this, here, now—has me on the edge. It's not right. It's so terribly wrong.

"Open. Relax," he says gruffly. The pressure intensifies. He's going to do this no matter how much I struggle and cry. So why struggle? I can't help crying but I can let go.

I can let go.

I fall onto the desk, letting it take all my weight, and I think I hear him whisper good girl. Angel. Brat. You don't know what you do to me.

He pushes the head of his cock inside and I'm dying. I'm going to die. It's a painful stretch, too big and too much and yet not enough. Hades plays gently with my clit. It's the polar opposite of what he's doing to my ass. My legs shake. I'm up on tiptoe, trying to get a good angle, trying to relieve any of this intense pressure, but nothing works. The trembling moves up and takes me over. I'm at its mercy, and his.

Another inch. Another.

"Good." His voice is stretched thin. "Good, you filthy fucking thing. You're such a pretty liar, such a pretty thief. You're doing so well. Hold still. Yes. Hold still, that's it—"

My mind splits away from the rest of me. He is so huge, and I am so small. Another inch, and then another. He keeps me from falling. That, and the desk. One by one, my memories fly away. The things I wanted. My name. I'm no one. I'm his.

When he's fully inside of me I know it's the end.

The end of me, the end of the world, the end of everything. If he moves I'll die. The stretch is too much, the struggle to keep letting go is too much.

Hades doesn't move.

He makes me do it.

His fingertips on my clit have gone still, and I only notice because he starts moving them again in an infinitely soft circle. "No," I howl into his empty office. "Don't make me."

"Oh, Persephone. It's far too late for that."

One final stroke yanks me down into an orgasm so filthy and powerful that my eyes go dark from all the tears.

"Please, please." I sound like I'm underwater, drowning in him. "Please." I don't know what I'm begging for.

What I get is Hades dragging himself back out and pushing himself back in. He sets his own deadly rhythm and I twist in his tie, searching for his hand, and when I find it he doesn't shake me off. Hades holds on tight while he fucks the breath out of me, and then the tears, and then, finally, lets himself go. "Fuck," he says, so softly I could be imagining it, I could be hallucinating it. "Fuck, I love you."

23

SOMEHOW, we end up back in Hades' bedroom. There must be a...a doorway, a hall, a secret passage, because I have no memory of hundreds of people staring at me, draped half-naked in his arms. Then again, maybe they did. Who cares? I'm untouchable now. He's done his worst, and I survived. I just can't keep surviving. I'm distantly aware of a shower and then riding him, my fore-head pressed against his neck, and then I'm dead to the world. See you when spring comes.

His voice wakes me up. It winds its way down the hall to the bedroom and brushes over the shell of my ear until I'm forced to unbury myself from the sheets. It's a wild tangle in the bed, which makes sense given what I can remember of last night.

Somehow, miraculously, I'm not hurt. A flower rests on Hades' pillow—one of the purple ones that grows outside, near the ravine. Diamonds, and now this.

It's early enough that the window still displays faded stars. That means the sun will be up outside, and Eleanor will be working on her flowers. The floor is cool on my feet, enough to wake me up.

In the bathroom I catch myself with a stupid smile on my face. I might have been out of my mind but I could still hear him. I hear everything he says. In that moment it couldn't have been anything other than the truth. The flower proves it. The flower, the book, the jewelry...all of it.

Wrapped in a light blanket—more of a shawl, really—from the closet, I go out into the sitting room. It's empty, which is weird. I could've sworn I heard Hades in here. But since he's obviously not, I open the door and listen.

My stomach sinks. Hades didn't sound close because he was in the sitting room. He sounded close because he's yelling. What I should do is stay where I am and wait for him to come back, but I can't. It'll squeeze the air out of me and make my hands shake and honestly, no. I'm not going to do it.

The voices come from his office. Oliver's first. "I'm not fucking with you and—no, no. My people aren't fucking with me. This is happening."

It stops me dead center in the hallway, and I have to catch my breath. Oliver sounds afraid. And I know he wouldn't talk to Hades like this unless that fear was real. If Oliver's afraid, then I should be afraid. No question.

Something crashes against glass and cracks it. I get one hand up to cover my head before I manage to take hold of myself. It's easy enough to ignore the outside world when I spend all my time helping Eleanor in the garden and getting dragged into Hades bed. His presence doesn't leave a lot of room to dwell on what's happening out there— with Zeus, with my mother, with anyone. Her fields and his whorehouse seem like they're a million miles away. The moon has more of an effect on our lives.

Okay. New plan. Don't sneak up on this conversation, which is obviously not going well. Just walk like a normal person. My nerves stop me from taking heavy steps. Also, it's extremely difficult to make noise in bare feet. Not trying to hide will be enough.

"This is untenable," Hades hisses. I can see it now —he's probably got his knuckles against the surface of his desk. I've got to get in there now before they stop talking and he finds me out here. A few more steps, a little more speed—

That tiny burst of speed is how I end up stepping in front of his office door at the moment Hades rubs a hand furiously over his eyes. It's how I'm there to see the words come out of his mouth. "Fuck, Oliver. I should never have accepted her as payment from Demeter."

The world stops. Collapses into itself. Detonates. Or maybe that's just my heart. I can't move, or speak. Hades twists toward the window in his office.

I see him see me in the reflection and turn, fast, too late.

"Persephone—"

My bare feet help me with the dead sprint back down the hall and to that outer door. I don't know what's worse. There are so many horrible things carving themselves into me that I can't tell which one deals the killing blow and makes me cry. Again.

The door leading outside opens for me, flooding the end of the hall with pure sunlight. Fuck him—I'll go where he can't go. I'll stay in the light forever. See how he likes it, see how he likes how this feels, if he could even feel this. It's agony. Heartbreak overflows into all of my veins. I can't outrun it. My only solace is that, this once, I can outrun Hades.

My toe catches on an upturned chunk of dirt, throwing me off balance. For a second I swing toward the ravine. It would be a terrible fall. Let it happen, something inside me says. Just let it happen.

No.

I'm better off living in hell than dying in a fucking ravine.

It's not just him. It's not just the fact that he lied yesterday and I believed him. This wild keening that I can't stop is also for my mother. Why does it hurt so much? I knew—I always knew—

I hold my breath but more sobs tear free. There's no holding it back, no stepping away. A stark breeze dries the tears on my face and whips my hair into my eyes. More tears come to replace them. I can't decide whether the sky is an uncaring witness or a friend. The sky—a friend. I'm losing it. I always knew my mother didn't love me the way parents in books loved their children. She just didn't, or couldn't. But I never thought she'd sell me out. For what? For what? There's no answer on earth that can fill in the hole, newly blown, where my heart used to be.

Someone's talking to me but I can't make out the words—Eleanor. She comes hurrying across the grass. I'm too far gone to be embarrassed about how ridiculous I look right now in this shawl, with no shoes on.

"Persephone, darling, what's the matter, tell me—" Her question cuts off in a gasp. She raises her voice. "Don't do this, Luther. She'll be back in a minute."

He stalks across the grass, eyes steely and dark. "Go inside, Eleanor."

"I'll bring her—"

"Go inside."

Eleanor squeezes my shoulders and steps back. I

feel her go. She won't be far, I can tell...but she's an old woman, and I'd rather fall into the ravine than ask her to stand between me and Hades.

"You don't know what you heard," snaps Hades. "Running out here like this is a stupid fucking idea, Persephone. You are asking for punishment and I'm happy to give it."

"You bought me? My mother s-sold me?" God, it hurts so much.

He looks down at the ground and I know, with complete certainty, that this is his one concession to being out here where he should not be. This gesture is not about feeling ashamed. It's about staying alive. Hades picks up his head and looks me in the eye. Tension builds in his shoulders. If he hadn't stabbed neatly through my heart I would feel for him. But he did, and I want this answer for free.

"Years ago. Before you were born."

I thought there was nothing left of my heart to break, but there is. There's so much more. I stuff the back of my fist into my mouth to hold in the sound, swallow it back. "That can't be." I clear my throat. "I've spent my life—I've spent my life trying to get away from her, and she never wanted me to leave. She would never do that. She's obsessed with me. She loves me."

Never is a long time.

"That wasn't always the case."

Couldn't he just lie to me, for once? And say that she did love me at all? He's so mean. He's so awful. He's right.

Conor comes tearing out of the doorway in the mountainside, barking at the top of his lungs. Hades keeps his eyes on mine as Conor races around him in a tight circle, his barks softening, begging. He puts a hand down on Conor's collar and Conor sits, but I can tell he hates it. He struggles against Hades' legs, even with his own wound, and barks.

"Then all those papers I signed were meaningless. Fake. It was never real."

Hades points a finger at the door. "Get back inside."

The only reason I go toward the door at all is because Eleanor shouldn't have to watch this. I want a closed door and several feet of rock between me and the rest of the world. But when I get there, I can't go in. I turn on the spot and block Hades' path. Conor pulls urgently at his collar. I'm ready to scream forever, just keep screaming until I'm dead, but somehow it becomes words. "I'm not going anywhere until you tell me the truth. I'm done with lies, Hades. I'm done with buying everything I need to know about you, it's not fair."

"You want the truth?" He advances on me, caging me in, his face a mask of pain and frustration. This is the first time he's ever looked how I feel. "You've always belonged to me. It was only ever a matter of summoning you."

How many more knives, how many more cuts? When am I going to blessedly bleed out? If it happened now I could at least see the sky. "I thought you wanted me," I hear myself say. I sound crazed. I feel crazed. I'll float away and disappear any moment now. "I thought you cared."

"That's the fucking problem." He backs me up until I'm flat against the unyielding rock of the mountain. "Loving you is like staring into the sun. You're a liability, Persephone, and you always have been. To everybody." Conor moves out of his position in a black blur and forces himself between us. "Get the fuck out of my way, Conor." Conor snaps back at him, teeth out. His body shakes against my skin.

I get one more breath and then, because I can't leave and I can't stay, I squeeze between Conor and the wall and go back inside. I don't look back.

24

HADES DOES NOT COME to find me in the guest suite, and at first I don't care. I've cried so hard that I'm sick, or at the very least I've damaged something. My stomach, maybe. It hurts. Everything hurts. I curl up on the bed in a dramatic pose because it's the only thing that seems right. Let him do what he's going to do. I don't care.

The minutes tick by, turning to hours. At some point I must fall asleep because it's dark the next time I look.

And he's still not back.

Maybe I killed him. Not directly, obviously, because that's impossible. But maybe...

My sad, stupid heart seizes the thought and won't let it go. Eventually I heave myself off the bed and tug the shawl around my shoulders. I look terrible —I can feel it. Puffy eyes. Red cheeks. Nobody's going to care. I don't care. I'm not really awake.

Hades is nowhere in his private rooms. It takes me twenty minutes to look inside all of them, my horror growing with every tick of the clock. Why can't I just not care? If I could stop caring, everything would be so much easier. I wouldn't care that we've had a fight and somehow he won. I'm not sure how, but this doesn't feel like winning. At all.

No Hades. No Oliver. I check over my shoulder at the main doors, but nobody's there. Nobody's watching. I'm alone.

I'm not staying in here to wait for my fate. I'm done with all that. Whatever's happening is outside the double doors.

Voices—thank god. I push away the sense of relief. There's no earthly reason to be relieved that he left me in there to wait out that horrible silence. What comes at the end? A train ride back to my mother's fields? No. I'll figure something else out. Anything else. I'll walk if I have to. That feels better—an inkling of a plan. It's definitely not a good plan, but it's a direction.

Hades has a meeting room.

He probably has more than one, but the voices lead me to this one, a space in the hall between the rotunda and his rooms. A crowd of people— ten or twelve—has gathered around a long meeting table. It's all dark, like everywhere else he spends time, but a glowing light in the center of the table illuminates all of them. Hades stands at the end of the table, Conor by his side. The dog doesn't like this. Neither does anybody else.

Hades sees me in the hallway. Conversation filters out. Words like weapons. Words like bombs. These are things that have to do with war, not business. I want to melt back into the shadows and disappear, but screw them. I'm part of this, too. Until I can pack up and leave, anyway. But before I leave, I'm going to find out what they know.

Oliver catches my eye on the way into the meeting room and nods. It untwists some of the anxiety at the core of me. Approaching Hades does not. He has a boundary around him now that I won't cross.

The invisible walls around him feel as real as the mountain stone.

I stop a foot away from him and listen. Nothing these people are saying makes any sense. Maybe this is still part of a dream. "What's happening?"

Hades leans back in his chair, watching them but answering me. "Zeus and Demeter have formed an alliance. They're moving on the mountain."

"Why would they do that?" My mind is thick with heartache and grief. "You said that I...belong here. That she signed me away."

He doesn't blink. "She did."

"Then why are they coming here? For you?" I pull the shawl tighter. Too tight.

Hades's jaw works. "If people honored the terms of their contracts, none of this would be a problem, would it?" He meets my eyes with a glare. "Demeter offered you in exchange for services I provided." He keeps his voice low. The others in the room keep talking amongst themselves. They're being so courteous while I die all over again. "That's how all of this started. This is why we're in this fucking mess."

Across the table, Oliver says something to one of the other men and his sentence ends with the word *attack*.

I'm awake. I'm wide awake now. An attack. They're not talking about a figurative attack, they're talking about a real one. They're talking about killing and damage and casualties.

And...there's a lot to attack here in the mountain. A lot that I love.

It hurts to know that and I push my fists over my heart to counterbalance the weight. It wouldn't hurt if it wasn't real, and it is. Because somehow, somehow, I've fallen for this place. For Oliver and his scar and his crossword puzzles. Eleanor and her flowers.

And Hades, who I hate. And love. Two sides of one coin.

"I'm yours now," I whisper. "Why are they attacking?"

Hades looks at me, not a shred of blue visible in his eyes. I don't even know how he's upright. A current goes between us, through the empty space. He keeps his hands close to him. He won't touch me.

What if he never touches me again? The thought fills me with loss.

"Your mother changed her mind."

He lets me sit with it—stand with it—for long enough that my heart tumbles onto the floor. And then he turns away.

"Go wait in your room, Persephone. Lock the door."

"No."

That would be easy. It would be so easy to go back to my room and cower in my bed and pretend this isn't happening. But it *is* happening. And these aren't just his people anymore. They're mine.

"Show me the plans." I overshoot it, too loud, but the people closest to me at the table notice. Then the next ones down. "Show me *now*." Hades watches me, but I don't look at him. "Faster than that." It feels right to say it, an edge in my voice.

Oliver's the first to get up and once the dam is broken the rest of them follow. There's a brief scuffle over who gets to put the plans in front of me —a schematic of the entire mountain, including the train station. The only inaccurate part is Hades' private quarters. He wouldn't let them survey that, apparently. I guess I'm not surprised.

"We have the women and children going out to the train now." Oliver draws a finger from the space by the mines—it must be housing—to the train station. "We have an emergency car. They could get—"

"No. *No*." Think. I've read a lot of books about war, which my mother found preferable to anything with love or tenderness or escape. "Don't send them out there. You'll lose all of them." The train track is a giant circle. Sending them out is sending them into my mother's territory, and Zeus's. They'll panic, they won't stay on, and if they get out into my mother's property they won't come back. "Don't send them toward the train station."

"Where, then?" Oliver holds up a hand to someone else at the table. They're not making plans for the future. This is right now. What I say will change—or ruin—people's lives.

"Up." I tap quickly on Hades' private rooms. "Bring them up, right now."

Oliver looks at Hades over my head. He must get some kind of approval because a man behind him jumps up and runs out. Focus. Hiding isn't enough.

"How close are they, Oliver?"

"Minutes." He checks his watch. "Maybe less."

I trace down the plans until I find what I'm looking for—a room labeled ARMORY. "Do you have charges?"

"Yes."

"Is someone down there now?"

"We have people waiting."

The room has gone quiet around us. I feel ancient. Like an ancient warrior queen. I wonder if all ancient warrior queens secretly felt like frauds but ultimately had to keep going anyway.

"You have to fill the train station with charges. That's the biggest entrance. But it's not the only one, is it?" The plans confirm this. There's a secondary stop for the train, and there's the mines themselves. "No. Charges at both stations. If anybody else is down in the minutes, have them shoot out the work-lights. What about outside?"

Two of the men at the table exchange a glance.

"What's that supposed to mean?" There's no time

to be a shrinking violet right now. "Is there something out there?"

One man clears his throat. "We...acquired automatic weapons. Through back channels."

"Send people there. Right now. Are you closing the station doors?"

"Now," Oliver answers. "There are backups, but if we blow them apart they won't hold forever."

"Forever is a long time," I tell him.

Oliver looks at me, and I wait for him to tell me this is the craziest idea he's ever heard. That it won't work. That they're just going to bleed people out of the mountain like they planned and hope for the best. "Thank you," he says finally, sounding sincere. Maybe a little surprised.

Everyone looks a little surprised.

They must have been waiting for this, because the few people who have been sitting leap up and the ones who were standing run for the doors. They divide all of my orders neatly between them, and in the space of thirty seconds they're gone from the room. Heavy footsteps recede down the hall and Oliver yells for someone to *go faster*.

It's me and Hades now, alone in this room.

There's nothing to look at in the plans now—everything is in motion. But he's still here. I look up into his face and find his eyes glowing with approval. With possession. I was stupid before, thinking I would ever leave. If I live through this, I never will. If.

He goes from the room then, crossing the hall into another room, this one mostly glass and screens. From here we can look down on the mountainside. The gates at the front edge of his property seem closer now. There are people there. A *lot* of people. Those gates won't stay closed for long.

I reach for Hades' hand, hoping against hope.

He takes mine back and lifts my knuckles to his lips. *This could be the last kiss,* I think. A *boom* sounds somewhere below us, horribly loud through meters of rock. Another *boom.*

"They're here." I squeeze his hand and watch the people at the gate hurry. They're frenzied. Fierce. We're under attack—our mountain, our family. Our love.

He squeezes back.

THANK you so much for reading SUMMER QUEEN! This breathtaking trilogy concludes with MIDNIGHT KINGDOM, available May 2020.

Revenge is a dangerous game, but I played it for Persephone. Now we're locked in battle with a lethal enemy. I own her body and I'll win her heart. But with enemies at the gate and my fortress under attack, there's something more at stake—our lives.

Order MIDNIGHT KINGDOM now!

Need another forbidden romance right this instant? Try my epic best friend's little sister romance with a scorching military hero in BEFORE SHE WAS MINE!

Download BEFORE SHE WAS MINE, free everywhere!

For more books by Amelia Wilde,
visit her online at
www.awilderomance.com.

Printed in Poland
by Amazon Fulfillment
Poland Sp. z o.o., Wrocław

58370619R00148